One, Wizard Place

SENTINEL

BY

D.M. PAUL

COVER ART BY JAY EPPERSON

INTERIOR ILLUSTRATIONS BY FRANK BERGER

This is a work of fiction. The events and characters described here are imaginary and are not intended to refer to specific places or living persons. The opinions expressed in this manuscript are solely the opinions of the author and do not represent the opinions or thoughts of the publisher. The author represents and warrants that s/he either owns or has the legal right to publish all material in this book. If you believe this to be incorrect, contact the publisher through its website at www.arcticwolfpublishing.com

Re-printed 2008 Arctic Wolf Publishing

Arctic Wolf Publishing
http://www.arcticwolfpublishing.com

ISBN-10: 0-9817472-0-5
ISBN-13: 978-0-9817472-0-0

Printed in the United States of America

This book is dedicated to my wife and daughter, for their continued love and support.

Special thanks go once again to my editing wizard Deanna Brady. She can be found at getwords@getwords.net or getwords@gmail.com

Book 1 - One Wizard Place
Book 2 - Sentinel
Book 3 - Sidhe

Visit

www. onewizardplace.com

This book is dedicated to my wife and daughter, for their continued love and support.

Special thanks go once again to my editing wizard Deanna Brady. She can be found at getwords@getwords.net or getwords@gmail.com

Book 1 - One Wizard Place
Book 2 - Sentinel
Book 3 - Sidhe

Visit
www. onewizardplace.com

CONTENTS

PREFACE
Nine Years Ago

ONE
Cloudview (Almost the Present)

TWO
Sharp Blade

THREE
Birds of a Feather

FOUR
Nargoyle

FIVE
The Isle of Demise

SIX
Shadow Lizard

SEVEN
Spiders

EIGHT
Black Dragon

NINE
Drago

TEN
Escape

CONTENTS

ELEVEN
Nawg

TWELVE
Dragons and Ogres and Wolves, Oh My!

THIRTEEN
Just Business

FOURTEEN
Getaway

FIFTEEN
Enob

SIXTEEN
It's Elementary

SEVENTEEN
The Age Of Doom

EIGHTEEN
Deep Below the City

NINETEEN
Distraction

TWENTY
The Wyrd

EPILOGUE

-Preface-

Nine Years Ago

Fox Strongbow lay awake in his bed, staring at the ceiling. A pale yellow glow framed the outer edges of his closed window shade, indicating that dawn was quickly approaching, but this wasn't what had awakened him.

The young elf sensed change in the air. It was more than just a bad dream that wrenched him from his slumber; it was the stone-cold realization that the life he knew was about to change. Although most long-lived adult elves barely acknowledged his existence at only seven years of age, Fox knew that he was more than just an ordinary elven boy.

Fox was faster, stronger, smarter, and more emotionally mature than most other elf children. He was keenly aware of the world around him and could read its subtle energies, even at his young age. These gifts enabled him to live just an instant faster than the rest of the world. He could perceive things coming before they happened and react instantly to events as they transpired.

It was this special perception that woke him, as if the air itself was charged with an unseen electrical current, a subtle shift in reality that confirmed his suspicions. The boy tried to dismiss the dark thoughts, but there was no shaking them. He knew with complete certainty that at any moment the waves of fate would crash into his life and change him forever.

It was just after dawn when Fox's father, Arlyn Strongbow, awoke to a knocking on the front door of his house. He pulled himself out of bed and looked over at his slumbering wife, Maeve. She murmured something in her sleep and rolled over onto her side but didn't wake.

Arlyn slipped quietly out of their bedroom and eased the door closed behind him. He made his way down a narrow hallway and padded silently into the main living area of his home. Just as he reached the door, he noticed that his son was sitting silently by himself in the dark living room. The boy was fully dressed and had a small leather pack beside him.

All sorts of thoughts raced through Arlyn's

mind, but before he had a chance to voice them, their visitor knocked once again. Fox looked up at his father with a grim expression on his face and gestured to him to open the door. Arlyn obliged, unbolting the lock and grasping the cold metal handle. He pushed open the door but found nothing more than long shadows that stretched outward onto his front lawn.

Then the open doorway shimmered, and the air in front of Arlyn rippled, reflecting the morning light at strange angles. Unexpectedly, two hands seemed to emerge from nowhere, pulling back a suddenly visible hooded cloak. The hood had completely concealed the visitor's face, and when it fell away Arlyn immediately recognized the man who had been hidden under the cowl. The visitor pulled his arms free of the garment, revealing the rest of his body. He checked that the cloak was fastened securely around his neck, then flung it behind him and allowed it to hang down his back in the manner of a great, shimmering cape.

Arlyn stared at the man standing in his entranceway but couldn't comprehend fully why he would arrive there so early in the morning. He heard a soft cough coming from over his shoulder and turned around. It was his son, who now stood a few feet behind him, fully dressed and carrying the small travel pack.

Arlyn looked back and fourth between Fox and the visitor, suddenly comprehending the magnitude of the situation. His heart sank as he gestured for the man to enter his home. When he closed the front door, he looked over to his son, who hadn't moved an inch. He nodded to Fox, and they made eye contact for what Arlyn knew might be the last time for a long while.

In that moment both of them came to grips with the situation and relaxed ever so slightly, understanding that they couldn't control what destiny had in store for them. Arlyn looked away first and nodded to his visitor without saying a word, gesturing for him to take a seat in the living room.

The visiting elf stepped silently over the threshold and into Arlyn's home, his great cloak hanging behind him, shimmering and shifting colors with every move he made. He seated himself on a leather couch and waited for Arlyn and Fox to follow.

After they were seated, the visitor looked Fox in the eye and spoke. "My name is Eldin. I'm the King's personal guardian." He then turned his attention to Arlyn. "I believe you know me as a Sentinel."

Arlyn nodded. "Yes, I've heard of you and know your position, but what does this have to do with us?" He had already guessed the answer to the question but simply wanted to delay the inevitable.

Eldin turned back to Fox. "I've been watching your son for some time now. He's more than just a simple boy. He has abilities that other children do not have… but I'm sure you're already aware of that."

A door opened on the other side of the room, and Maeve appeared. Arlyn met her gaze and replied, "We know. We've known for some time now. We also knew that it was just a matter of time before others realized… but I'm surprised it has come to your attention so quickly."

Eldin smiled slightly. "I'm the last of the Sentinels. For generations our numbers were strong, but in recent years there have been no children born with the gift. Our members have dwindled to only myself. In order to continue our tradition, I need an apprentice." He paused for a moment. "Your son has the gift. He's the first in more than a hundred years."

Fox's mother seated herself next to her husband. They looked at each other, clasped hands, and turned to their son. "What do you think about all of this?" Arlyn asked Fox. "Ultimately it is your decision."

Fox smiled. "I think fate has just crashed ashore."

His parents just looked at him, perplexed. "What?" asked Arlyn.

"Nothing, really… just a joke." He paused for a moment and looked to Eldin again. "What exactly does this mean--what do you have in store for me?"

Eldin glanced back and fourth between Fox and his parents. "Training. Lots and lots of training--nine, maybe ten years of it, to be followed by a lifetime of noble service to our King."

He looked for a reaction from Fox, but the boy didn't even blink. Eldin wrung his hands. "The next nine or more years of your life will consist of the most intense schooling imaginable. Your body will be pushed to its physical limit every day. Your mind will be filled from the moment you wake to the moment you fall over in sheer exhaustion."

Eldin shook his head from side to side as if he

could somehow soften the truth, then continued. "I will begin by teaching you the most fundamental steps in hand-to-hand combat, slowly advancing your skills until you discover the underlying principle in each technique. Eventually your skill will be honed to reflect maximum efficiency in the uses of physical and mental energy. We will cover the major categories of throwing, grappling, and striking techniques. Then we will combine what you have learned so that your unique method of self-defense will be equally adaptable to and effective against a single attacker or several.

Eldin gave everyone a moment to let this sink in. "During this time you will also become proficient in the use of every conceivable weapon our arsenal has to offer. Based on your skill level, you will choose a weapon that you wish to master. You will train with that weapon every day until you reach perfection."

Eldin hesitated, then continued. "Most important, you will develop an inner strength, a power that fuses both mind and body… a strength that can sweep away everything before it."

Eldin looked at the boy, who hadn't moved. "Does this not stun you? I wish I could offer you a carefree childhood, like so many other children your age will have, but your gift has singled you out from the rest of the world." The visitor smiled a half smile. "I can offer you this… at the peak of your physical and mental abilities you will be the single most powerful tool the King has in his arsenal. You will have no equal."

Fox's mother began to weep quietly, and his father put an arm around her as they gazed at their young son. The fact of the matter was that it hadn't really come as a surprise to them. Once they had realized that he had the gift, they had known this day would arrive. It seemed that Fox had already come to grips with it.

The boy reached down and grasped his pack. "I don't suppose I have a real choice in the matter, so I might as well face the inevitable."

Eldin stood up. "You always have a choice."

Fox stood as well. "Do you seriously believe that?"

Eldin frowned. "No… in this case, I suppose I don't really believe it either."

Fox went to his mother and father and hugged

them both. "Will I be able to stay in touch with my parents?"

This time Eldin was able to smile broadly. "I'm not an ogre! Most of your training will take place here within the kingdom of Greylok. Your parents can visit our quarters as often as they wish."

Fox nodded to Eldin. "I'm as ready as I will ever be, so we may as well get started."

Eldin bowed his head slightly and made for the door. As he pushed it open, sunlight streamed through the opening, and he walked out of the house. Fox turned and hesitated for a moment, as if to apologize to his parents for leaving, but then followed his new teacher obediently.

Arlyn and Maeve stood at the threshold and watched their son disappear down the road. The young elf turned one final time before he was out of sight and waved goodbye to his home and family and to the carefree life he had known.

fb
© 2006

-Chapter One-

Cloudview (Almost the Present)

C*RRZAAP...!!!!*

The electrostatic energy blast exploded across the wall of the building and left a large crevice in the smooth, polished granite surface, right next to the howler. The fleeing creature looked at the result of the misplaced shot and grinned nastily. Smoke from the burn began to irritate its nostrils, and it wrinkled its flat nose at the smoldering hole and glowered back at the two law enforcement agents in pursuit.

Agent Murdox looked at the glowing cavity with distaste and turned to Kase, his young partner. "Nice shooting, Texas," he jeered. "Now you've just managed to make it angrier."

Grinding its massive claws right into the stone, the howler climbed vertically up the wall before turning its cat-like head toward the shooter and his partner. The creature gazed down at the pair with its six fiery red eyes, and its grin turned to a ferocious growl. The beast howled into the night, opening its maw wide to expose a mouthful of razor-sharp teeth.

Kase pointed his Berrington Model 13 electrostatic energy gun at the howler a second time. He had it set on *Stun* so that it wouldn't kill the creature--just knock it out of commission for a few hours… he hoped. Although it could cause some real damage to hard metallic surfaces, the weapon was designed just to overload the beast's neurological system and send it into a static state of shock.

Murdox dropped back a few steps to stand behind the boy. "Try to hit it this time."

Kase looked back at him and smirked. "Wow, I never thought of trying that... I'm sure glad you're here to offer such great advice."

Justin Kasey Hobskin, whom everyone called "Kase," was an agent with the Incantation Enforcement Agency, Counter-Curse Division, in the city of Cloudview. Kase's father, Brent Hobskin, had created the Counter-Curse Division years earlier to correct magic that went awry and to undo curses that needed to be rectified. For years Brent and his closest friend and partner, Murdox, had worked the cases together until the fateful day when they were attacked with an evil witchdoctor's dark magic.

In a heroic attempt to protect his partner from a powerful curse, Kase's father had dived in front of Murdox, partially blocking the spell. The incantation had been intended to transform both men into mindless beasts, but only Brent had received the full force of the attack. Because Brent had absorbed the majority of the evil energy, Murdox was only partially affected.

On that day Brent Hobskin was irreversibly changed into a wild wolf, with no trace remaining of his former self, while Murdox was only transformed physically into a wolf-dog but retained his memory, identity, and self-awareness. The magic had changed his body, but he retained his mind, soul, and--to everyone else's great dismay--his less-than-charming personality.

After that day, Brent's young son had taken up his father's role. Fortunately, in a world of too many bizarre creatures to name, no one had found a human boy to be of any special interest or concern. Murdox had stayed with Kase, and they had been partners at the division ever since. In fact they had turned out to be a pretty good team and had become well respected within the agency.

Unfortunately, today was the Counter Curse Division's day to help eradicate some of the city's more hostile inhabitants. Cloudview was not just an ordinary city; it was actually several cities in one. Technology and magic had evolved together here, creating a colossal structure more than a hundred levels high. Each level was actually an entire city in itself, with an overwhelming assortment of multistory buildings of every conceivable shape and size.

Regrettably the city was tremendously overpopulated, with a wealth of both beneficial inhabitants and the inevitable bad seeds. Over time the city had attracted the usual nocturnal predators, who found that they could prowl there as easily as they could in the outside world.

The seemingly never-ending food sources brought these creatures there by the droves, and the problem soon became epidemic. The situation was soon too much for local exterminators to handle, so city officials brought in the Incantation Enforcement Agency to help. After a recent troll and ogre uprising, though, many of the employees who usually handled this task were off work on medical disability leave.

Inevitably volunteers were selected from each of the departments to provide assistance. Thus, the time came for the Counter-Curse Division to lend a hand... and a paw, in their case. Seeing as Kase and Murdox were the only two employees in their division, they were lucky enough to inherit the job.

Howlers happened to be among the more troublesome local pests. A howler weighed between 200 and 300 pounds and had the body of a jungle cat, but with six legs instead of four, all designed for climbing and fighting. Howlers were nocturnal predators and had perfect night vision in six fierce eyes that were arranged vertically, three on each side of the head. Their dense fur coats shifted in hue between slate gray and black, which made them nearly invisible in the shadows. To make matters even worse, they had the unique ability to scale vertically up and down buildings by adhering to the walls with their powerful, ultra-sharp claws. The creatures utilized this skill to capture their prey, dragging unsuspecting victims high up into aerial dens from which they were helpless to escape.

Fortunately, most of the howlers had been eliminated from the city, but enough remained to cause trouble for the locals. This one in particular was tricky and had eluded capture for some time. It watched the two agents for a second and then hissed and turned, deciding to use the moment to escape instead of fight. Although the wolf-dog must certainly have looked like a nice potential snack, the howler's belly was already full, and it didn't feel like wasting any more time.

The two agents tracked it to a dead-end alley that stank of rubbish and decay, cornering it on the back wall just above a pile of overfilled trash bins. It leapt off of the wall and sailed over the agent's heads, landing gracefully in the deep shadows behind them.

Kase spun around and fired his pistol. The blue energy beam discharged from the weapon and slammed into the spot where the beast had been a moment before. The creature howled in pain, and Kase thought he must have hit it; but instead of it being knocked out by the blast, it leapt off the ground and hung from the building, nearly a dozen feet up the side wall.

Murdox snarled. "I think you hit it in the tail. Great! Now you've really made it mad."

Kase watched the beast scale the wall, and sure enough--the end of its tail was pulsating with blue static electricity and smoldering slightly.

"Ooops!"

"Shoot it again before it gets away!" Murdox yelled.

Kase fumbled with the gun for a moment and then fired again at the beast, but it had already taken off running sideways down the passage, holding fast to the alley wall. Kase slammed his weapon back into its holster, and the two agents took off running after it.

-Chapter Two-

Sharp Blade

Fox held himself motionless as he watched five swordsmen encircle him. They smiled deviously and converged around the apprentice, all pointing sharp-bladed weapons in his general direction.

In an instant Fox appraised the situation and allowed the attackers to tighten their ring. The points of their blades inched closer and closer, but an instant before they could tear into the young Sentinel, he propelled himself upward, leaping out of the center of the circle. He landed silently just outside the group and lashed out with his own blade, striking one of his foes just behind the knee. The older swordsman fell on his face, and the remaining attackers regrouped and rushed the apprentice. Fox leapt to his feet and instinctively defended himself from a blow that came straight at his head.

Fox allowed his attacker's sword to slide down the blade of his weapon until it rested against his hand guard. He then rotated his arms in a circular motion, twisting his attacker's wrists in the process. When his assailant was significantly off balance, Fox pulled upward with his blade, yanking the sword out of the other fellow's hands. He finished off the attack by reversing the blade's direction suddenly toward the now-unarmed attacker and striking his assailant in his side, knocking him to the ground.

Once again his remaining adversaries tried to regroup and circle around the young apprentice. To their dismay he instinctively blocked their forward progress, and at the same time, slid forward, positioning himself against the back of one of the attackers. As the next blow came at him, Fox stretched out his arm in a curved extension, dipped his head toward his chest, and surged forward in a single circular motion, proceeding along the arc formed by his arm.

As he rolled away from the group, he thrust his sword behind him, protecting his body from any outside interference. When his roll came full circle, he sprang upwards, pivoted on his heels, and reemerged on the opposite side of his foes.

Before his opponents realized what was happening, the blow that was originally intended for Fox tore into the side of the attacker against whom he had been positioned a moment before. This knocked the man down, and he fell to the ground with a yelp. Fox took advantage of the situation and slammed his blade into the fellow's backside before he was able to pick himself up off the ground, effectively taking him out of commission.

Of the original five assailants, only two now remained. They whirled in place and repositioned themselves to face the young apprentice. Fox regained his composure and followed through with his weapon, bringing it to a stop in an upright position. He relaxed his stance ever so slightly and faced down the remaining attackers.

A short distance away, under the concealing canopy of an apple orchard, Eldin watched the battle unfold. He reached up casually, plucked a ripe piece of fruit from the nearest tree, and tossed it in the air to measure its weight. In one swift motion he hurled the apple at Fox. He was a master, unequaled in the fighting arts, and the apple sailed through the air in a streak of red, directly on course for his young apprentice's head.

Fox didn't even blink. Years of practice had provided him an acute awareness that instantly alerted him to the danger. He shifted his center of gravity slightly to one side and moved his neck no more than an inch from its original position. In the same moment, he repositioned his sword at a slight angle and directed its motion in order to deflect the incoming projectile. An instant later the apple slammed into the wooden blade of Fox's practice katana and splintered into hundreds of wet fragments.

In that moment of confusion, the two remaining attackers came at Fox with full force, but the apprentice sidestepped their attack and shifted his body into a spinning motion, whirling his sword on a central axis while the blade traced a dynamic sphere in the air. Everything happened in a smooth, gentle, circular motion, his response blending seamlessly with the attack.

Fox felt power well up inside him as he led the

attack away from his body while allowing himself to continue on a circular path. This sent his adversaries off balance, and he utilized the moment to finish them off. With perfect precision he continued rotating his body away from the attack as he simultaneously moved his weapon into a horizontal position. As his body came full circle, he pushed outward with his arms and slashed his katana into the attackers' exposed blades. He allowed his inner energy to flow outward into the attack, compressing the raw energy into the blow. His wooden blade tore through his attackers' swords, cleaving their blades in half and sending splinters in all directions.

Fox manipulated the situation instantly and brought his release of energy under control. He slowed his attack in order to limit the damage to his assailants, but allowed it to continue through the rotation until it smashed into the closest opponent's thigh. Even though the force of his attack was controlled, it still dropped a man to his knees in agony. Instantly rebounding off the blow, Fox spun in the opposite direction and whirled his blade into the final attacker, lifting him from the ground and knocking him onto his back.

Eldin saw it all and smiled.

He's ready.

Fox grabbed a quick bite to eat before dragging his weary bones back to his sleeping quarters. It had been just over nine years since Eldin had initiated this rigorous training schedule, and in that time the young elf had learned more than he could ever have thought possible. Though only in his mid teens, he had the knowledge of a scholar many times his age. His body was lean and fit, without an once of excess fat. His training had evolved through many aspects, and ultimately it had succeeded in fusing his body and mind to a degree that allowed him to operate at a level far above his peers, both physically and mentally. At this moment, though, none of that mattered. He just wanted to slip into his bed and rest before another day of agony.

As he turned the corner and headed down the narrow hallway that led to his quarters, Fox noticed a thin band of light around the door. As he approached, he sensed a presence in the room, but this didn't trigger a sense of alarm. He already knew who was waiting for him and thought, *Can't he just let me have a moment's peace?*

He pushed open the door and spotted Eldin standing beside his bed. His teacher was wearing drab gray trousers, dark leather boots, and a loose-fitting, washed-out, green pullover shirt. There was nothing unusual for this time of year... so Fox hoped that maybe he was just there on a social visit. *Sure!*

He scanned his teacher from head to toe, trying not to give away his feelings. Eldin was physically fit and rather tall, as elves went. For all the years Fox had known him, he'd preferred to wear his long hair tied back. Only recently had he allowed it to hang loose. Fox's master looked like a typical elf: sharp-featured, with dark, almond-shaped eyes and slightly pointed ears. Fox didn't know Eldin's age, but when they'd first met more than nine years before, his hair had been dark black. In the past few years, it had gradually begun to turn silver, indicating that he was aging. This didn't mean that he wasn't still a formidable foe. Even a bit long in years, he was still the most deadly weapon the King had at his disposal; but Fox never failed to point out to him that he tired slightly faster than he had in the past--a subject that always got his goat.

Eldin ushered the boy through the doorway and gestured to him to sit in a leather chair in the corner of the room. Fox fell into the seat and wondered exactly what his teacher had in store for him now. Eldin folded his arms across his chest and shifted his weight from one foot to the other, allowing his apprentice to sit without saying a word to him.

Eldin smiled at the boy who had come so far since they had first met. Fox was sixteen now--hardly a drop in the bucket in elf years--but was far more than simply a young male. Physically he was near perfection. Fox was healthy and strong, muscular, yet limber. Over many long years, his arduous training had allowed him to develop both his physical strength and his inner strength of character to their utmost capacity.

Eldin couldn't help but be pleased. His apprentice had grown into a handsome, polite young man, and he felt like a surrogate parent. Physically, Fox was elf through and through. He was of medium height with long dark hair, pointed ears, and as with most elves, a deceptively small frame. Only his eyes differentiated him from others of his kind. He had gray eyes, but Eldin knew them to be windows to a complicated soul. He was generous and honest. He did what he was told and only argued when necessary. Eldin couldn't have asked for a better pupil, and Fox may very well have been the best student he had ever seen.

Eldin nodded his head in satisfaction. Fox's training was complete; there was nothing more he could teach him. The rest would simply have to come from experience.

Fox looked up at his teacher. "What brings you to my humble abode?"

Eldin smiled and glanced out through the open door. "Oh, not so much. I just have a little present for you."

Fox was surprised. This wasn't what he expected. The few times his master had visited him in his personal quarters had been when he had done something wrong or had needed to partake in extra training. Fox was exhausted and hoped this wasn't some kind of a trick, but Eldin didn't often play cruel jokes on him.

They both looked up when a stranger knocked

lightly on the door. Fox recognized the face but couldn't place his name.

Eldin grinned and ushered in the visitor. Fox noticed that he was extremely top-heavy in a muscular way, and he seemed very old, even for an elf, as indicated by his long gray hair and slightly stooped posture. The stranger had broad, thick shoulders, enormous chest muscles, and massive arms. Such physical proportions were unusual in elves, who normally had long, lean, light, and flexible frames. The only elves Fox knew of who looked stocky worked as blacksmiths in forges.

With this realization, Fox was able to put a name to the face, then gasped in awe. This stranger who had walked into his room so casually was a legend among his people.

With other races, elves have a reputation for creating exquisite, finely crafted weapons. Without a doubt this was true, but even among their own race elves whispered of a legendary smith who could create weapons of such craftsmanship that anything he shaped was held in the highest esteem.

Why was he standing in this room? Fox

wondered.

The apprentice leapt from his seat and stared at the venerable smith. He carried with him a piece of oilcloth, which was wrapped around a long, thin object that appeared to be just under three feet in length.

Eldin shook the smith's free hand and then looked over at Fox, who approached them both. "I'd like to introduce you to Taurnil." Eldin grinned as he saw the reaction on his apprentice's face. "From your expression, I see that you recognize the name."

Fox simply nodded in response and shook the famous smith's hand. Strangely, his fingers felt soft and delicate, not hard and calloused as Fox would have expected.

They all stood in silence for a moment before Eldin spoke again, looking directly at Fox. "Today was the last day of your training. There is only one task left for you to do."

Fox's eyes grew wide, and he glanced back and fourth between the two adults. He shook his head to clear it and tried to grasp what he had just heard. "Do you really mean it?"

Eldin patted his apprentice on the shoulder with

one hand and signaled to Taurnil that it was time. The smith obliged and handed the oilcloth to Fox, who slowly began to remove the wrappings. When he had unwrapped the cloth, he found within its folds a sword sheathed in a black obsidian scabbard so dark that it seemed to absorb the light around it.

The sheath was unembellished except for a sigil in the shape of a stylized fox head, which had been embossed approximately three quarters of the way to the scabbard's mouth. At first the mark appeared to be the same color as the scabbard itself, and he thought he had only noticed it because of its slight variation in texture. When he examined it closer, however, it looked more like a shadow, subtly shifting through graduated shades of black as he turned the weapon over in his hand.

Fox looked to the two men for approval, and they both nodded back. He grabbed the handle. The grip was unadorned, wrapped only in black leather with fine silver thread woven through it. He pulled the blade from the scabbard with hardly a whisper. As the tip of the blade pulled away from its sheath, Fox felt a surge of energy course into his hand, flow through his arm, and plant itself firmly within his body. He looked at Eldin and Taurnil for an explanation, but the two men only smiled, so he shook off the strange feeling and continued to examine the weapon.

He shifted the sword from hand to hand and examined it at arm's length. It was flawlessly balanced and felt like an extension of his arm. He scrutinized the blade more carefully but could find only perfection. It was single-edged and crafted with a shallow curve in the style of a Samurai sword. The blade itself was not grooved and was long enough to be considered a katana. It was polished to a mirror finish and had a slightly bluish tint. A distinct deep-black temper line ran down its cutting edge in an irregular wavelike pattern, signifying that the blade had been hardened throughout, rather than just at the edge.

The blade itself ended in a triangular black hand-guard that seemed to be crafted from the same material as the scabbard. Just above the guard, located on the collar, was a carved fox-head sigil identical to the one on the scabbard. When Fox saw it, he laughed to himself with glee as he realized the significance of the carving. The sword itself was actually created for him.

Eldin looked at his apprentice. "It's yours. You and I are the only two Sentinels left, and I want my partner to be well-armed."

Fox grinned from ear to ear. He didn't know what else to say, so he simply said, "Thank you." He turned to Taurnil and bowed. "Thank you for creating such a masterpiece."

Taurnil returned the bow ever so slightly. "The blade is unbreakable, and the edge should never dull. I dare say it may be the finest sword that these hands have ever crafted. Use it wisely."

Eldin gestured to Fox, and the apprentice handed the sword to his master. Fox felt a sense of loss the moment he relinquished the weapon--it actually felt like he was missing a part of himself.

Eldin examined the weapon. "This is more than just a sword. The weapon is now a part of you. I saw your expression when it bonded with you." He hefted the blade and extended it outward at arm's length. "Practice with it tonight. Channel your energy into the weapon, and you'll be pleasantly surprised to see the result. Use it as an extension of your body."

Fox nodded, just beginning to understand what he had acquired.

Eldin handed the sword back to the young apprentice and turned to the master smith. "Thank you. As always, you've outdone yourself."

Taurnil turned to the young elf. "Good luck, Fox. I expect to hear great things about you." Then he bowed and stepped out of the room.

Eldin shut the door behind him and turned his attention back to Fox. The apprentice sheathed his weapon and carefully wrapped it again and placed it in a drawer.

"You have one final task. It will be your final test as an apprentice, but because of the nature of the test, we will go together."

Fox looked up at him, narrowing his eyes. "And so it begins."

Eldin smiled.

-Chapter Three-

Birds of a Feather

Eldin took a seat on the bed and looked Fox in the eye. "Rest tonight... you're going to need it. Tomorrow we're heading out for an extended journey south."

Fox eased himself into a nearby chair while Eldin shifted in his seat, making himself more comfortable.

"Your sword isn't the only mark of our trade. You will need a cloak similar to mine. As I'm sure you have already learned, it's much more than just a piece of clothing--it can keep us alive when times get really tough."

Fox knew that he was referring to his Chameleon Cloak. It had the ability to camouflage the wearer to the degree that it made him nearly invisible, as well as protecting him like a suit of armor. He had trained with Eldin's many times and was quite proficient at using it.

Eldin relaxed slightly and leaned back on his hands. "It's one of the major components that provide us a strategic advantage over our foes. As far as I know, only Sentinels utilize this natural technology. What I am about to tell you is not to be repeated."

He hesitated for a moment to let the instruction sink in. "There is an island far to the south, nearly three days' flight from here. On that island exist two creatures that possess the key elements of the cloak. The first creature is a reptilian predator similar to a lizard, but it stands and hunts upright on its hind legs. For lack of a better name, we call it a Shadow Lizard. Its skin has millions of tiny reflectors and refractors that bend and return light in such a way that it can mimic its surroundings perfectly. When the creature remains stationary, it effectively becomes invisible. Its natural camouflage works so well that even when it moves, it's hard to see… just a shifting distortion that is nearly impossible to spot. The skin also absorbs heat energy, making it invisible to predators that track the heat signatures of their prey.

"Fortunately for us, this beast sheds its skin as it

grows. It then collects the discarded skin and uses it to cover its nests. We've found that the creatures don't move these nests very often over the years, and after generations they've become thick with skins. The nests are nearly invisible and just about impossible to find, but the Sentinels that went before us have painstakingly mapped out a few of them, and we should be able to find one of them easily enough. It isn't going to be a walk in the park, though--we'll have to be diligent and keep a wary eye out for them. A Shadow Lizard is larger than a grown man, with a mouthful of sharp teeth and claws like daggers. They can be vicious--we don't want to tangle with one if we can avoid it."

Fox had a million questions but allowed his master to continue.

"Our first mission is to collect the skins, but the second adventure is even more fun. Once past the lizards, we'll head farther inland and within the realm of the second creature's lair. These beasts are the source of a material that is essential to a cloak's construction. They live underground in caverns toward the center of the island; specifically they reside in a dormant volcano that is littered with ancient lava tubes. Within these tubes live the spiders... big spiders--really big, nasty spiders."

Fox gulped out loud. "Great... I hate spiders!"

Eldin smiled. "I know you do, and so do I, but this particular spider is very special. Its silk is the strongest material known to exist. Ounce for ounce it is many, many times stronger than the most resilient elven steel and is almost weightless. A few strands of this spider's silk can lasso and halt a full-grown dragon in flight."

Fox's jaw dropped in wonderment.

Eldin sat upright on the bed. "The cloak is woven with a combination of the lizard skin and the spider silk. This combination makes the cloak nearly invisible, as well as virtually indestructible."

He looked over at Fox's new sword. "Once it's constructed in the traditional way, I doubt even your new sword could cut through one. It took us generations to figure out how to process the raw materials into the cloaks we use. Eventually our ancestors discovered how to piece them together and utilize the finest qualities of both materials. In the end we have a garment that keeps us hidden from our enemies, as well as armor that protects us from their weapons."

"The cloak isn't magic?"

Eldin smiled. "No, it's just a perfect combination of naturally occurring elements. Because it isn't magical, you'll have to be trained to use it properly. Once you have one of your own, we'll train with it until you're really comfortable in it. The important thing to remember is that even though few weapons can damage it, that doesn't mean the blows won't hurt. A strike won't pierce your skin, but a solid blow will still break your bones."

Fox nodded. "That makes sense. My best course of actions is to avoid being seen altogether, and if I can't, I'll still need to evade an attack"

"Now you've got it."

"So where do we go from here?" Fox asked.

Eldin stood and reached for the door. "Pack a light bag for a trip south. Expect to be gone for at least a week. I'll meet you tomorrow morning about 8 A.M. in the roost. We'll fly out from there." With that he opened the door and left his apprentice to review what he had just learned.

The next morning, Fox awoke excited to start the day. He had spent an hour or so the night before practicing with his new sword and packing for his trip. By 7 A.M he was dressed in lightweight brown breeches, a comfortable pullover shirt, and a sturdy pair of leather boots. He slipped his pack over his shoulder and headed for the huge kitchen to gather food for the trip and grab a bite to eat before they left.

The Sentinels had never had an offsite annex to house their company. Because of the nature of their job, they had always resided within the walls of the castle, and their proximity to the King made their job all the easier. As a courtesy, the King had a small wing constructed to house them more comfortably, separated physically from the castle by a narrow breezeway, but still part of its overall structure.

Within half an hour, both his pack and his stomach were full, and he made his way back to the Sentinels' wing. He walked back through the lavishly decorated halls of the castle until he came to a narrow corridor that ended at a heavy wooden door. The door opened to the covered breezeway that connected the castle to the much smaller structure that stood separate from the main building.

Fox took a final look around the dwelling before making his way out the door to a steep set of stairs that lead to the roof. There a large roost had been constructed to accommodate the huge birds that the Sentinels use for transportation around the kingdom.

Elves utilize various forms of transportation to travel the vast kingdom of Greylok. Over thousands of generations, the capital city had been constructed to blend seamlessly into the Great Forest, hidden from all but a select few. The city itself was built high into the canopy of the trees.

The builders had molded the canopy in such a way that a vast open plain was created by allowing the branches of the trees to grow together as a foundation. On this foundation they were able to build large cities and towns far above the forest floor. The cities were interconnected by an infrastructure of roads and highways that were designed to accommodate a wide variety of creatures and modes of transport.

In general elves preferred living creatures over inanimate technology as a means of transportation, and they utilized various beasts of burden for traveling these forest byways. At any given moment, all types of tree-dwelling creatures could be seen, some pulling carts and wagons while others were ridden, used solely for the purpose of transporting people.

Sometimes the elves used relatively small, agile birds for faster commuting, but outside the protective canopy of the forest, dragons and giant raptors ruled the sky. Only the Sentinels dared travel on feathered wings beyond the protection of their leafy home, and over countless generations they had raised and trained giant predatory birds that had become their mounts for long-distance travel. These were fierce flying steeds, and only a few had been tamed for this use.

In past generations, the rooftop roost might have housed as many as fifteen giant raptors, but now only three nested within its walls. They were penned in large, comfortable habitats where they were fed and looked after meticulously.

Fox climbed the stairs to the roost and emerged into a beautiful morning. The air had a slight nip to it, and he slipped his hands into his pockets. He traversed the straw-covered roof until he reached the stable that housed the birds. The stable itself was old, but well kept. It was constructed of stone and dark timber, with two massive doors marking the only entrance.

He unlatched the doors and slid them open, allowing sunshine to illuminate the interior of the building. Eldin hadn't yet arrived, so Fox decided to get both his own and his teacher's birds ready for flight. Eight large pens lined the walls of the building, with one on the southern wall converted into a tack room for riding gear. Fox looked in on the birds, but the morning light had only just brought them out of their slumber. He decided to gather the appropriate harnesses and other gear for them both from the storeroom and place it just outside the stable in two neat piles.

His teacher's bird was an enormous elder hawk. He was by far the largest mount in the roost, with a wingspan nearly thirty feet across. The bird had a short, dark, hooked beak, expansive wings, and a broad tail. Predators of this size were long-lived, and Eldin's bird was only just reaching middle age, with a long service history still left in him. He was a beautiful creature, all brown except for a swath of white that extended from his chin all the way to his belly.

The bird watched Fox with dark, penetrating

eyes as the young apprentice unbolted the gate to his pen and approached the magnificent beast.

Fox bowed slightly to the creature. "Hello, Morwen. How are you this morning?"

Eldin had named him after a great warrior that had served with the Sentinels ages before.

"Your master will arrive shortly, but until then, would it be all right if I brought you into the sunshine and readied you for a long journey?"

The birds would usually allow only their masters to get close. Fox wasn't sure just how well the birds understood, but they were extremely intelligent creatures and seemed to know exactly what their masters were thinking. Very few other people could actually communicate with the massive predators, but Fox had a way with animals, and Morwen was no exception. The bird trusted the boy nearly as much as he trusted his master. He gazed at the young apprentice intently and nuzzled him gently with the top of his beak.

Fox smiled and led the creature from his pen and into a large holding area where he had placed the riding gear. "Just wait here, and I'll get Stormwise. You two can chat while I rig up your tack."

Fox headed back into the stable and reflected on how he had come by his own bird. It had been about five years ago that he and Eldin were on a training exercise at a rocky coastline site a few days' journey from Greylok. They had been standing on a bluff overlooking the ocean when they'd spotted three dark shapes flying their way. A gyrfalcon nest was located on the cliffs not far from where they were hiding, and the intruders apparently knew this, as well. Fox and his teacher immediately took cover and watched events unfold.

The dark shapes turned out to be green dragons interested in the clutch of eggs the falcons were protecting. They heard rustling from below the cliff line and watched as two massive falcons flew off to intercept the trespassers. A fierce battle unfolded before their eyes, but the two watchers were helpless to intercede. Blood and feathers filled the sky, but in the end the falcons were simply outnumbered. They fought desperately to protect their young, but it was a loosing battle from the start. Both birds were killed in the struggle, but not before they had mortally wounded two of the three dragons. The third dragon, however, was able to slip through the battle and steal the unprotected eggs.

When the dragon had flown out of sight, Fox decided to investigate the nest, just in case it had missed any eggs. That's when he heard frantic chirping from somewhere below the nest. Apparently one of the baby falcons had already hatched and had slipped from the nest during the struggle with the dragons.

Out of true concern for the creature, Fox brought the baby bird up to where Eldin was waiting. Only a few days old, she was already nearly as big as his arm. She was a beautiful little thing, but helpless without a mother or father to provide for her. Needless to say, it would have been a true shame to let her suffer any more after surviving such a horrific encounter with the dragons. They decided to bring her back to Greylok and raise her themselves. The knowledge that the hapless creature would die without their intervention helped to justify their decision.

During their return from the cliffs, the bird was strangely quiet until they were about a day away from home. As the early evening approached on the second night from the coast, the little bird started to cry. She whined and chirped frantically toward the sky. By then they were under cover of a dense forest. At first they thought she was just hungry or missing her family. When they entered a clearing and could see that the sky to the south had turned black, they realized that a violent storm was approaching. If the little falcon hadn't warned them, the storm would have been on top of them before they even realized it was coming.

The little company took shelter in a cave and weathered one of the fiercest storms to hit the area in a long while. They decided then that their new little friend should be named Stormwise, and she'd been called that ever since.

Fox opened the gate of the enclosure that housed Stormwise and gently stroked the side of her head. She had grown into a beautiful bird. She was whitish-gray, with a dark mask and fine, slate-gray bands on her belly, legs, and tail feathers. Her black-tipped wings were swept back and pointed. In combination with her long split tail, they made her a swift, aggressive flyer--faster than the other birds in the roost and among the fastest in the world. Morwen exceeded her in size by quite a margin, but her unique wings and smaller stature made her better suited to weaving through the forest canopy, and as a pair they made an impressive team.

Fox led Stormwise away from the pen and into the holding area, where Morwen was waiting. Eldin had arrived while Fox was retrieving her and had already begun saddling his bird.

Fox stopped a few feet away. "Good morning."

Eldin reached down under Morwen and cinched tight one of the saddle straps he had just set up.

"Yes, good morning to you. Sorry for my tardiness, but the King waylaid me. We're going to have to make haste on this mission. It seems that the border trolls are getting restless again. When we get back, His Majesty wants us to run a little reconnaissance mission and find out what exactly has got them all riled."

Fox nodded without comment as he lifted his saddle into place and began the process of rigging up his harness.

Within fifteen minutes the two Sentinels had saddled and packed their gear onto the birds, and for safety they checked each other's equipment. They then left the two birds to rest a moment while they headed into the storeroom to put on their riding clothes.

Fox glanced at Eldin, who was pulling a pair of leather riding pants over his breeches. "Do you think it will be all right to use just the lightweight chaps and gloves? I'm thinking of forgoing the heavy jacket and sticking with only what I've got on. My logic is that if we're going south, it's just going to get warmer."

"Yes, I agree. I'm just going to wear the pants and gloves, myself." Eldin adjusted his pants so they were comfortable and grabbed a pair of gloves and yellow-tinted goggles from a nearby shelf. "The weather isn't too bad now. We'll try to stay low when we leave the Great Forest, and the temperature should remain comfortable. I don't want to lug along the heavy jacket either… it just slows me down."

Fox nodded and slipped a pair of amber-tinted goggles over his head as they went back to their mounts. After checking their gear one final time and making sure their weapons were within easy reach, they each grabbed hold of their saddles, slipped a foot into the stirrups, and heaved themselves onto the birds' backs.

Eldin made himself comfortable in his seat and glanced back at Fox. "I'll take the lead. We're going to head southeast through the Great Forest. That will put us at the western edge of the Swamp of Doom and Despair. If we had time, we would skirt around it, but unfortunately we don't have the luxury. Once over the swamp, it will be a short hop to the coast. On the coast we'll take another bearing and head for a small island that's about a day's journey out to sea. The island is midway between the coast and where we need to be, but I don't want to push the birds any harder than necessary. We'll rest on that little island and fly the final leg the following day. If all goes well, we should be on the Isle of Demise in just under three days. It should take us only a day or so to get what we need there and another three days to return. We should be back here within a week."

Fox collected the harness reins and eased Stormwise next to Morwen. "Doom, Demise, Despair… such encouraging names…!"

Eldin smiled and released the tension on his reins, gently prodding Morwen in the sides with his heels. The giant bird lifted his head to the sky and began to run. He then spread his massive wings and leapt effortlessly into the air.

Fox urged Stormwise to follow. Without hesitation she bounded forward and launched herself into the sky. She spread her wings and climbed away from the roost as they raced after the big hawk.

The young Sentinel tightened his grip on the reins, and a slight turbulence buffeted him as he urged his bird to match pace with Morwen. She dipped her wings gracefully from one side to the other as she banked around massive tree trunks in search of a clear passage through the forest. Fox watched the ground drop away beneath them as his bird accelerated after his teacher's.

-Chapter Four-

Nargoyle

Kase and Murdox followed the howler as it raced down the narrow passageway, its claws tearing holes in the smooth, polished walls. Breaking free of the alley, it leapt from the wall, landing on the street with a thud. The two detectives weren't far behind, and they hit the street at a run. Fortunately for them it was late in the evening, and only a few pedestrians were out and about.

The creature took off down the road, easily leaping over a parked vehicle that stood in its way. Kase and Murdox followed as best they could, but the boy had trouble keeping up. Murdox had the advantage of four legs and could almost keep up with the creature, but he slowed to let Kase keep pace with him. They followed the howler until it raced across the street and slipped down another alley.

A hover car whizzed by in front of them,

stirring up a cloud of dust and preventing the two agents from following down the alley right behind the creature. The agents stopped at the curb, and Kase grabbed his knees, out of breath and panting.

"Whew! I don't think I can keep up for much longer."

Murdox looked up at the boy. "Don't worry. It's gone down a dead end. It's either going to turn and face us or scale the wall, up where we can't reach it anyway." The wolf-dog looked toward the alley and sniffed at the air. "You'd better get the gun out, though. I don't think it's interested in doing any more running."

Kase turned and faced his partner. "You're just a ray of sunshine, aren't you?"

Murdox smiled in the way that only a dog can.

The wolf-dog gave the boy a moment longer to catch his breath, and the two agents carefully crossed the street. It was fairly late in the evening, but the city was still buzzing with life. Even though the street they were on wasn't hopping with activity, the sky above them was filled with aerial traffic. Kase looked up into the night sky and watched as innumerable vehicles cruised between the buildings and merged into the mass of commuters on the skyways.

Murdox looked up at the boy. "I know what you're thinking. 'There they go, cruising by overhead, oblivious to our plight here on the surface. Not a one of them realizes that we're down here risking our very lives to keep their city safe, just so they can go about their petty little lives without worrying about what's going to jump out of the shadows.'"

Kase looked down at the dog. "No. I wasn't really thinking that at all. Actually I was wondering when the agency was going to give us a hover-car so we wouldn't have to keep running around all the time. My feet are killing me."

Murdox shook his head. "Oh, yeah… me, too. That's exactly what I was trying to say."

Kase just shook his head, too tired to comment.

They stepped into the alley. Kase took the lead with gun drawn; Murdox sniffed at the air and pushed him along in the right direction.

The howler was at the end of the alley, perched on the wall about ten feet in the air. Tensing its muscles to pounce, it watched the two agents as they approached.

Kase and Murdox stopped a safe distance away, and the young agent raised the gun to fire. The howler stared at the boy, its six red eyes glowing in the dim light. Suddenly the street lamp at the end of the alley flickered and died, casting the two agents into deep, shifting shadows. The sounds of the city died away, and the alley went deathly silent. In the darkness, goose bumps crawled over Kase's arms, and the hair on the nape of Murdox's neck began to rise.

A moment earlier the air was warm and calm, and now a cold breeze blew through the back street, bringing with it a stomach-turning stench that filled their nostrils: the odor of death. Kase retrieved a flashlight from his backpack and switched it on.

In the silence a drop of water fell nearby, and in that moment both agents understood the meaning of fear. The pale yellow beam cast light onto a creature that truly looked like something straight out of a nightmare. Standing between them and the back wall of the alley, the beast vaguely resembled a towering humanoid in shape. It had huge, bat-like wings with massive clawed hands and feet. It wore a tattered black cloak, concealing most of its muscular body. What little flesh was visible appeared to be chiseled from stone, covering its frame like armor.

The creature pulled the hood from its head, revealing a demonic face adorned with long, curved horns like those of a ram. It smiled, revealing a mouthful of fangs that dripped what must have been venom. A dark aura of power surrounded the beast, and it gazed at the two agents from soulless black voids where its eyes should have been. It carried with it a long wooden stave on which a wicked-looking, three-pronged, barbed spearhead gleamed in the flashlight's glow.

The partners had all but forgotten about the howler. Then it hissed at the new arrival, and the dark creature turned away from the terrified agents and focused its attention on the six-legged beast they had been chasing.

Too frightened to move, the howler clung to the wall at the back of the alley. There were few creatures that could scare a howler, but this new predator seemed to do a pretty good job of it. The demon watched the howler for a moment and seemed to snuffle at the air. It lifted its stave and poked the weapon at the beast, bringing it back to life. No longer scared motionless, the howler snarled in response.

Kase raised his pistol and pointed it at the new arrival's back. "Don't move, or I'll be forced to shoot," he said in a small, squeaky voice.

The demonic-looking monster ignored the boy and continued to provoke the howler with its stave.

Kase took a small step forward and spoke with a little more authority. "I'm warning you! Stop what you're doing and drop your weapon, or I'll be forced to shoot."

The creature spun around like lightning, swinging its stave at Kase and forcing him to stumble backwards. The boy fell to the ground, accidentally discharging his weapon at the demon. A blue beam erupted from the gun, and static energy encircled the creature.

Technically speaking, a Berrington Model 13 was an upgrade from the previous Model 12. Both models were capable of completely overloading the neurological system of a full-grown ogre or troll. The only difference between the two weapons was that the Model 13 was a tad more reliable. Needless to say, the effect of shooting either gun should leave a victim unconscious for a few hours. In this case the blast only annoyed the creature slightly because its cloak began to smolder at the edges.

The monster took a step toward Kase and grabbed the pistol from the young agent's hand. It looked it over for a moment before pulverizing the weapon between its massive palms. The creature waggled one long, stony finger in front of the boy's face, then dropped the smoking pile of metal and fused electronics in a small heap at his feet.

Without another thought, it spread wide its wings and leapt into the air. As it accelerated diagonally upward, it stretched out its legs, and using the talons on its feet as hooks, casually tore the howler away from the wall and carried it away effortlessly into the night.

Murdox watched as the beast departed the area. "I think I soiled myself."

Kase was staring at the smoldering bits of pistol at his feet.

"Ditto."

-Chapter Five-

The Isle of Demise

The Sentinels were tired after a full day on wing. The Great Forest loomed miles into the sky behind them like a vast mountain range, and the sun had just disappeared behind the towering trees, casting the two riders into shadow. An hour earlier they had flown beyond the border of Greylok and out from under the protective forest canopy. They knew that flying outside the elf kingdom was dangerous business, but to be exposed after nightfall would be suicidal.

Daylight had just about run out, and they decided it was time to set down for the evening. With Eldin in the lead, they were skimming a few feet above a dense pine forest. In the fading light, they could just make out the edge of the Swamp of Doom and Despair, a few miles in the distance.

Eldin slowed Morwen and allowed Stormwise to match speed beside him. He gestured to Fox and yelled over the wind noise.

"I don't want to put down in the swamp… it's just too dangerous. I know of a small clearing not far from here. We'll rest there for the evening and make an early start of it in the morning."

Fox signaled that he understood and allowed Stormwise to fall back behind Morwen.

Within moments the clearing came into view. Eldin led the two birds in a long, lazy circle to investigate the surrounding area before landing. When they decided that all was clear, he tightened his flight path and made a steep approach into the open field. The field was small, but the hawk flared open its immense wings, stopping its forward motion an instant before its talons gripped the soft, grassy turf. Stormwise landed silently beside him, her wings compressing the air in one final downward stroke before her legs absorbed the landing with hardly a shudder.

With only the faintest glow of daylight left, the Sentinels dismounted. Eldin and Fox had been working together for more than nine years, and they knew each other's routines well. Being so close to the swamp meant they were in hazardous country, and Eldin wanted to check the surrounding area for any sign of danger that they might have missed from the air. He unsaddled Morwen, then left his apprentice to unpack their gear and sort out the details of the camp.

Fox checked the sky and noted that it would likely be a cool, clear night. He glanced at Stormwise, but her mysterious internal barometer didn't seem to be alerting her to any weather-related perils. Under the circumstances he decided to spread out the bedrolls and simply camp under the stars with the birds tethered loosely nearby. There was a slight chill in the air, so he built a small fire and prepared a light meal in anticipation of Eldin's return.

Shortly thereafter, the elder Sentinel strolled into the campsite and seated himself on a fallen log a few feet from the fire. By then the sun had set, and a half moon was beginning to rise. He apportioned some food for himself and tore a piece of bread from a loaf that Fox had set out. He took a couple of bites and dipped the bread into the stew the apprentice had prepared.

"Nice! You're becoming quite the cook."

Fox grinned. "Yeah, I'm thinking of giving up the whole Sentinel thing and studying to be a chef instead."

Eldin ignored the quip and looked away from the fire. "The woods seem clear for the time being, but I think we should keep watch. This is dangerous country."

The apprentice looked up from his meal. "All right. I'll take the first lookout and wake you in a few hours when it's your turn."

Eldin nodded, and they finished the rest of the meal in silence. They relaxed for a time, simply listening to the sounds of the night. Fox drifted away from the fire and checked on the birds, but they had already fallen asleep, their heads tucked between their wings.

Fox climbed up and perched on a nearby rock overlooking their camp, wrapping himself in a blanket. Eldin slipped into his own bedroll next to the fire and fell asleep under his apprentice's watchful eye. A few hours later, they traded places, and Fox got some sleep.

Morning arrived with a light mist, and Eldin

soon shook Fox's shoulder gently. The boy woke with a shiver and sat up. He poked at the fire pit with a stick, but dew had settled over the area and saturated the ground, making the fire impossible to rekindle. He rubbed the sleep from his eyes and shuffled through his pack.

"We're going to have to eat a cold breakfast. I don't think I can get a fire started."

Eldin grunted and pulled some bread from his pack. Then he began to clear the campsite. Fox located a piece of cheese to gnaw on while he stashed his bedroll in his pack. He then finished packing the gear as Eldin went to check on the birds.

Eldin led their raptor steeds close to the fire pit. He stroked Morwen on the side of his head and glanced over at Fox, who was making the final preparations for their departure.

"Both the birds left camp an hour or so before dawn and returned only a few minutes ago." He examined their claws. "From the looks of their talons, I'd say they found breakfast on their own."

Fox glanced at Stormwise, remembering that although the birds could seem tame, they were still natural predators. He reminded himself that he and Eldin weren't vegetarians, either, although they were forced to breakfast that way on such days as this.

The sun had barely crested the horizon when they finished saddling their flying steeds. They completed their preparations, and Eldin looked over Fox's gear.

"By lunch we should be on the coast. We'll rest, grab a bite to eat, and let the bird's take a short break. If all goes well, we should finish off the last leg of our journey by early evening."

Fox nodded without comment and checked Eldin's rig for him.

The sun was barely beginning to burn through a layer of dense fog as Eldin and Fox found themselves winging their way over the Swamp of Doom and Despair. The swamp was fiercely dangerous, both above and below. The only safe route would be to avoid it altogether, but their limited time frame forced the two Sentinels to cross directly overhead.

Geographically the swamp was huge. It stretched around the northern border of the Great Forest and extended in a southerly direction for hundreds of miles until it enveloped a large portion of the forest's southern flank.

Eldin slowed his bird and matched pace with Fox. "We're fortunate to be crossing the swamp this far south. This is one of the narrowest points, and we should be halfway across within an hour or so... but don't let that make you overconfident. We still need to keep a sharp eye out. This is dragon country, and I want to make it across alive, so keep your bird low, and hug the treetops. Maybe we can avoid watchful eyes."

Fox nodded and watched his master return to his position at point. In unison both birds dipped their heads to the deck and dove downward to within a few feet of the trees, flying so close that their bellies were a few scant inches above the harsh swamp vegetation.

It was dangerous and inhospitable to flying. The mist drifting upward through the canopy enveloped them in the foul stench of the rotting swamp. It protected them from view of predators but left precious little room for error if an unseen obstacle crossed their path. They had little choice, however, so they coasted over the misshapen trees, thick with twisted vines and unchecked vegetation.

During a brief period when the almost ever-present mists cleared, they found themselves staring downward at stagnant black-water pools surrounded by endless fields of mud. The bones of hundreds of hapless creatures littered the surface, their decomposing bodies left to rot in the unforgiving climate.

It seemed that they might make it across when they spotted a strange-looking creature circling a few hundred yards away. The beast also spotted them and flew a little nearer to investigate. It made a fast pass in front of the two riders, close enough for them to get a good look.

Physically it was grotesque--about half the size of Morwen, with a mud-colored humanoid torso that was covered in reptilian scales. It had long arms and legs covered in the same thick scales, but where hands and feet should have been, it had birdlike talons. It flew on immense, oily black wings similar to those of a vulture, allowing it to stay aloft for extended periods of time.

The creature made a second pass, this time getting close enough for them to smell its fetid breath.

They were able to get a better look at its face and realized that it seemed almost human. They determined that *it* was actually a *she*. She had the face of a wretched old woman, with long strands of filthy green hair and fierce, hate-filled yellow eyes. She made a long sweeping circle around the two Sentinels, apparently deciding if they were worth the trouble to attack.

Instinctively Fox and Eldin reached for their weapons but hesitated before bringing them into view. The creature narrowed her circle and let out a horrific, cackling laugh that made the hair on the backs of their necks stand on end. Eldin motioned to Fox to come up alongside him.

"Hold your ground. I think that's a Manx. If I'm right, we might be able to pass without a fight."

Fox wrapped his hand around the hilt of his sword but resisted pulling it from its sheath. He knew what Eldin was on about. Manxes were close cousins to Harpies--violent, evil creatures with a taste for blood--but they also had brains and knew when not to pick a fight.

Long moments passed, but neither party made

any hostile moves. The creature circled around the two Sentinels, playing a deadly game of Chance. Then something stirred in the trees below and distracted her for a moment. Eldin took advantage of the situation and steered a course away from her. When she realized what he had done, she swung in close to him and hissed right in his face. Eldin pulled his sword halfway out of its sheath, making sure she got a good look at its shining blade.

The Manx made a cackling, hissing noise and then suddenly gave up the fruitless game and dove away into the swamp. A moment later she plucked an enormous snake from the stagnant waters and landed within the decaying branches of an ancient, lifeless tree. Fox caught a glimpse of her as she tore into the snake, still hissing and sneering at the two riders as they flew out of sight.

By noon the air was becoming fresher, and the perpetual fog of the swamp was beginning to lift. Within less than an hour they had spotted the coast, and their moods brightened. Eldin led the way, taking the birds in low over the rocky beaches until he spotted a suitable landing site. He located a familiar landmark and settled his bird into a gentle dive directly toward a large outcropping. Morwen glided over the jagged rocks and landed on a nearby sand dune in a spot where they would be partially protected from view.

The little company rested for an hour, basking in the early afternoon sun, and ate a light meal. For the sake of time the elves didn't remove the saddles from their birds, simply opting to loosen the straps and give them a short respite from the flight. Eldin pulled a map and a compass from his pack and took a bearing out over the ocean. He measured the breeze with his hand, then decided that it wouldn't be sufficient to set them off course.

When he returned his attention to the map, he noted that the island they sought was no bigger than a speck on the page, insignificant in the vast ocean surrounding it. It wasn't much more than a rugged atoll covered with a few scrub trees and a freshwater spring, but it would serve their purpose as a rest stop before the final leg of the journey.

Eldin showed the map to his young apprentice and explained the situation. Fox had flown out over the ocean before, but this kind of flying required complete confidence in one's mount. Fortunately the birds were exceptional navigators, and they would have no trouble finding land, even when none was in sight. Although magic and technology were often intertwined in their world, the elves preferred using their birds' natural abilities to any kind of equipment. Even the finest navigation tools would be hard-pressed to compete with the natural instincts of the birds.

Once satisfied, Eldin returned the map to his pack and nudged Morwen in the sides with his heels. The great bird took off with a leap and accelerated into the air. Stormwise followed without hesitation, and once again they found themselves winging farther and farther away from home.

Before long they had lost sight of land, and Fox found himself tracking vigilantly with a compass that was mounted in the horn of his saddle. They seemed to be on course, but he still felt a pang in his stomach when he thought of what lurked in the sea below him, just waiting for an unexpected gift from the sky. He willed himself not to give in to his uneasiness and settled himself into his saddle. Soon the gentle rhythm of Stormwise's wings made his eyelids lower, and he was lulled into a light sleep.

Hours had passed since they left the coast when a slight buffeting of the air awakened Fox. By now the sun was sinking toward the horizon, and they had only a couple of hours of daylight left. He checked his compass and noted that they still seemed to be on track, but he hadn't spotted the island they sought.

Eldin must have sensed his apprehension. He slowed his bird and flew in next to the young sentinel.

"Don't fret," he advised. "We should see the island any minute now."

Fox smiled, trying to hide any nervousness he might have revealed.

Eldin reached down and stroked Morwen on the back of the neck. "It's not much of an island, but it will be welcome enough after a day on wing like this."

Fox smiled and settled back in his saddle. In reality he didn't need the reassurance. He trusted the birds and Eldin's memory of the area, but it did bring him some comfort knowing that his backside would be getting a break.

Halfway Island soon came into view, just as promised. They circled around the small atoll as a matter of routine but spotted nothing that looked out of the ordinary. The island was small, perhaps a quarter mile wide by a half mile at its longest point. They located the clear-water spring near the southern end of the island, and Eldin swung his bird around to land on a large rock plateau adjacent to it.

The sun would set within the hour, so they hastily made camp in close proximity to the clear spring. There was no need to scout the island, so Eldin helped Fox with the birds. By nightfall they had set up a small camp. To Fox's relief the spring was fresh and clear, perfect for restocking their limited water supply.

The two Sentinels filled their water skins, built a small fire, and made themselves comfortable within the radius of its warm glow. They relaxed and took in the warm, clear evening, trying in vain to count the thousands of twinkling stars gleaming overhead.

Eldin looked up into the night sky as he spoke. "There's no need for a watch tonight. There isn't enough island to conceal any predators, and I doubt anything will come from the sea. Get as much rest as you can.

We'll need to be at our best for the next couple of days."

Fox poked at the crackling fire with a twig from the nearby scrub brush. He was eager to see what the next few days had in store for him… both excited and nervous at the same time. "I'll try my best to get some sleep."

Eldin smiled, lay back his head, and fell asleep watching the stars.

The night went by without issue. They woke before the sun had risen, ate a cold meal, and prepared the birds for the final leg of the journey. By daybreak they were on wing once more. The vast ocean spread out before them, nothing but a blue-green expanse of water as far as the eye could see. They were far to the south, and the weather was warm and wet. By midday a thundershower rolled in above them, drenching them to the bone, but the birds ignored the weather and flew onward toward their unseen destination.

It was late in the day before they broke free of the clouds again, and Fox realized that he was looking directly at the island they sought. It was just a speck on the horizon, but it was definitely land. Gradually the island came into view. It was big--bigger than he thought it would be. The foul weather they'd flown through was behind them, but a ring of clouds lingered around the upper reaches of the island, encircling what Fox knew to be a dormant volcano that was nearly completely shrouded from view.

Eldin led as they circled the island. It was lush and tropical, shaped in an irregular circle rising gradually out of the blue water like a green jewel. Sandy white beaches encircled the outer edge of the island, slowly giving way to a swath of dense rainforest. Toward the center of the island, the jungle diminished and the ground became rockier until an ancient, hollowed-out mountain rose out of it, shrouded by the cloud ring.

Eldin swung his steed inland for a closer look and to find a possible spot to land, but they quickly realized that the jungle was far too dense to allow for a safe approach. They circled for several minutes and made a few passes near the rim of the volcano, deciding in the end that their best course of action would be to land on the island's northern shore.

As the two riders guided their steeds into a

gentle approach to the beach, a flock of colorful little birds erupted from the thick jungle below, startling them. The raptors swerved to avoid the panic-stricken creatures, but the elves soon realized that it wasn't their presence that had created the sudden commotion. Eldin pointed to the jungle below, and they watched the vegetation shake violently back and fourth. They heard shrieks and cries from below the dense canopy as the jungle seemed to thrash below them. Before they could circle around to get a better view, all suddenly became silent again.

Eldin gestured to Fox to follow him to the beach, then caught a fleeting glimpse of the jungle shifting below him, as if a section of the trees were moving away from the commotion. A few minutes later, Morwen landed on the beach a short distance away from the jungle. Eldin watched as Stormwise set down nearby and waited for the falcon to settle in before dismounting and unpacking his gear.

-Chapter Six-

Shadow Lizard

Eldin shook Fox awake.

The apprentice opened his eyes and gazed around at the grim morning. During the night a thick fog had rolled in, and a light, misty rain had started to fall. He looked up at his teacher.

"I assume your watch went well?"

Eldin scanned the trees. "A few bumps in the night, but nothing of consequence."

They had made camp midway between the shore and the jungle the night before. Fox took the first watch and Eldin the second. It was now the morning of the fourth day of their travels, and they had just passed the night on the Isle of Demise. If all went according to plan, they expected to spend the entire day acquiring the items needed to fabricate the cloak and then leave for their return journey early the next morning.

Eldin pulled a light backpack from his gear and

assembled an assortment of weapons and food on the ground. He looked over to Fox to do the same. "Your test begins today. I assume you brought a small bag with you."

Fox nodded and withdrew a pack similar to Eldin's.

"Good," said Eldin. "Show me what you've brought along, and we'll determine what we need to take inland."

Fox did as requested. Eldin took a moment to survey what Fox had brought and seemed satisfied. Between the two of them, they had an eclectic assortment of food, weapons, and outdoor gear. Eldin stooped over his own group of items and plucked a metal tube from the pile. He unscrewed the top and withdrew a yellowed map that was frayed at the corners but still easily readable. He offered the map to Fox and let him look it over.

The young apprentice glanced back and fourth between the jungle, the shoreline, and the map. "Apparently this is a map of the island." He pointed to a few dots scattered at various locations on the map. "I assume these are nests where we can find Lizard skins."

Eldin nodded his approval and retrieved the map from Fox. He studied the ancient text and took a bearing from the sea and back to the jungle. "If I remember correctly, we should be in the right spot to head inland from here. If all goes well, we should be able to find an abandoned nest only a couple of hours' walk from here."

Fox looked over his shoulder and agreed with his master's conclusion.

Eldin took a final bearing from his compass and returned the map to its tube. He looked through his gear one last time and placed a few items to the side.

"Take a small portion of dried fruit and some water with you, but leave any meat behind."

Eldin looked over Fox's supplies again carefully and noted that his apprentice had brought along nearly the exact items he had. *Good boy*, he thought to himself. *He has anticipated the trip to the best of his knowledge, with little help from me.*

"Pack your sword, the rope, a small knife, and your compass. Anything else is up to you, but being sure to pack for stealth… and remember to leave room for what we need to recover."

The two Sentinels finished their preparations in silence and cleared their campsite.

Eldin watched as his apprentice finished packing and helped him arrange a few items in his bag.

"This island belongs to those that dwell here," he cautioned. "We are intruders, trespassers on their land. These creatures have done no harm to us, and I do not wish to do any harm to them."

Eldin hesitated for a moment, making sure that his apprentice had heard his words. "Your test is a mission of stealth. You have been trained to defend yourself and your King under all circumstances, but for a Sentinel, violence is a last resort. Typically many of our missions will consist of reconnaissance. You will go into a location, learn what you can, and get out without detection."

He looked directly at Fox. "This island is the perfect spot to test your skills. I already know you can fight, but I need to know that you can think on your feet in situations that could mean life or death to both of us. If you are to be my partner, I want you not only to defend my back, but what is more important, I want you to do your very best to keep us out of trouble in the first place. This island will test the very limits of your stealth abilities. If all goes well, we'll go in, get what we need, and get out. If we are successful, none will be the wiser."

Fox looked into the jungle and then back at his teacher. "I will do my best."

"I know you will."

Eldin finished filling his own backpack and then assembled the rest of his gear in a neat pile. He retrieved a large cloth bag that looked as though it had been dipped in a clear, thick coating. He packed the remainder of his and Fox's food in the bag and pulled the drawstrings tight. Then he placed the bag and the rest of his gear into his larger flying pack that hung on his saddle. He began to saddle Morwen and gestured for Fox to do the same with Stormwise. He lifted the big saddle onto his mount's back and cinched the belly straps.

"The Shadow Lizards are nearly blind… they hunt only by scent and sound, but don't be fooled by this. Even without sight they can track us flawlessly through the thickest jungle. Remember that their unique skin camouflages them perfectly to hide them from their prey. We'll need to be on our toes. If one picks up our scent, we might not know it's on our trail until it's too late."

He helped Fox with his saddle. "That's why I told you to bring only fruit and water on our trip inland. They hunt fresh meat. They're not scavengers, and I doubt they would be interested in dried fruit or attracted to its scent."

Fox nodded. He had already assumed as much but hadn't voiced his thoughts. "I'm curious, why did you wait until morning to conceal our food supplies in that bag?"

Eldin looked out toward the ocean. "We're fortunate that Shadow Lizards hunt inland. I suppose the sea air and ocean waves mask most of our scents and sounds. I've been told we are relatively safe at the coast, but I don't want to press our luck and take any further chances."

Fox pulled a strap tight under Stormwise. "That's why we're getting the birds ready to fly free?"

Eldin smiled. "Yes, that… but even if we are at

our best, anything could happen in the jungle. Any mistake could give us away, and a quick escape might be necessary. As I said before, I don't want to resort to violence. We're stealing from them... albeit only discarded skins and old cobwebs, but it's thievery nonetheless."

Fox finished packing his gear and readied Stormwise for free flight. Eldin did the same with Morwen, and soon the campsite had been cleared of their presence.

Eldin removed his sword and sheath from his gear and strapped it onto his back within easy reach of his hands. He looked over at Fox, who was doing the same thing. "Exquisite weapon you have there," he said.

Fox took a final look at his weapon, its sheath so dark that it seemed almost a shadow in his hands. All he could think of saying was, "Yes, it is. Thanks again." He strapped the sword to his back and pulled his backpack over it, tightening down the straps in the process.

Eldin bowed his head ever so slightly. "It's your due, for finishing your training, but today we'll see if you've truly earned it."

Eldin checked that Morwen was properly rigged before he gave him a firm slap on his flank. The giant bird spun its head nearly all the way around and let out a caw before it spread wide its wings and leapt away from the beach.

Stormwise sat silently, watching as the magnificent older bird flew away in a cloud of stirred-up sand. Fox smiled and shoved his bird gently in the side. "Go enjoy yourself. Just be ready if we call."

Without a sound she spun her head around and leapt away from the beach, chasing after Morwen.

Eldin patted Fox on the back. "I think I saw her smile." Then he turned to the young elf, and his face went serious. "Now, listen... the fun's over, and we need to get down to business." He checked his compass. "If we move inland on a northerly heading and manage to stay on course, we should run into a nest long before we reach the volcano. It should be old and unprotected, but we can't take any chances. These hunters are relentless. If they catch our scent, we'll be hunted down, tracked until we are forced to fight... and that would be a most unpleasant situation."

Fox didn't need to reply.

Eldin reached into his pack and withdrew a small glass vial. He carefully unscrewed the top and put a finger over the opening. He shook the bottle a few times and pulled away his finger, dabbing the liquid contents on his neck and the backs of his wrists.

Fox scrunched up his face. "*Whoa!* What is that stench?"

Eldin dabbed a few drops on Fox. "Most unpleasant, wouldn't you say?" He resealed the bottle and returned it to his bag. "That scent is the essence of rotted meat." He gestured into the jungle. "Our friends out there are predators at the top of the food chain. They hunt and kill only fresh game… and as I said before, they aren't scavengers. The scent of rotted meat shouldn't interest them much."

Eldin started into the jungle. "From this point onward, until I say otherwise, we must maintain complete silence. Everything you have learned up until now will be tested. The essence should keep our scents masked, but these creatures are equally adept at hunting by sound. It goes without saying that we are to use only hand gestures."

He turned and looked at his student. "You must reach out with your mind; attune your senses to detect the slightest disturbances in the air. Your skills and training are all you have. Use them so that we may pass through their domain like shadows, as quickly and as silently as the wind itself."

Fox scrunched his nose again. *Like a nasty, stinking wind,* he thought to himself.

Eldin pushed aside the dense foliage, and they slipped silently into the jungle.

About an hour had passed without either of them sensing danger when Eldin suddenly stopped in his tracks and raised his fist in the air. Fox was immediately alert to a tingling sensation that ran down his spine. He focused his attention on what lay ahead and felt a slight shift in the ambient pressure. Fox placed his hand on Eldin's back, acknowledging that he too felt the disturbance. They slipped behind the trunk of a large tree and hid between its roots. They peered into the distance, focusing on the thick foliage. Ever so carefully they reached out with their minds, probing the jungle ahead with the delicate fingers of their elven magic.

Nothing happened at first; then suddenly they saw the jungle shift ever so slightly ahead of them. They could barley discern the vague outline of a large creature. As best as they could judge, it was nearly nine feet tall, standing upright on two hind legs. It blended seamlessly with the surrounding jungle, and when motionless it literally disappeared into the background.

The two Sentinels instinctively slowed their breathing and became perfectly still. The beast lifted its head and snorted. Slowly it turned and looked in their direction, snuffling at the air and cocking its head from side to side. It moved toward them, stopping every few steps to listen and smell the jungle around it. Finally it stopped about ten feet away from the tree in which they hid and scratched at the ground with long sharp claws. Even at this distance, it was difficult to see, hardly more than a distorted outline only discernable when it moved.

They remained perfectly still, consciously forcing their physical beings to become one with the surroundings. Their breathing came in slow, controlled breaths as they shut down their bodies into a near-comatose state. The creature listened intently to the rhythms of the jungle, but the only sound coming from the two men was their hearts beating at a level barely discernable from the background noise, even to the most acute hearing at close range.

Many long moments passed as the creature snuffled at the air. Fortunately the wind was in their favor, and they remained downwind of the beast. A thrashing sound rang out a short distance away, distracting the creature. Finally it gave up the search at this location and lumbered off in the direction of the noise. They waited patiently for any sign that it might return, but it continued moving away from them.

Eldin gestured that they should move ahead, so they carefully picked their way deeper into the jungle. Gradually the canopy overhead became so dense that only thin shafts of light penetrated through the thick foliage. The lack of a constant light source had reduced the undergrowth to a few hardy ferns and ground fungus, making ground travel relatively easy.

They wound their way between the densely packed tree trunks, peering at the map and checking the compass from time to time. They had been traveling for about two hours like this when Eldin stopped and circled his finger in the air. He pointed to a spot where a series of rotting trees lay. They had long since fallen and had decayed to the point that only a few sections of the trunks hadn't sunken into the ground. A hole in the canopy where the fallen trees had once stood allowed light to penetrate to the forest floor. Taking advantage of the situation, a thick layer of undergrowth had claimed the warm, sunny environment. Now the former nest was overgrown with dense flora that included flowering vines.

The two Sentinels sat in silence for a minute, reaching out with their senses. They probed the air currents, sniffed the wind, and listened intently to the jungle. They let their senses reach outward in an ever-expanding bubble, feeling for the slightest disturbance and assuring themselves that there was nothing that might give away their presence. Nothing alerted them to danger, and they proceeded to the abandoned nest.

Quietly they removed the dense foliage to uncover the skins. At one time this nest would have blended perfectly with the dense jungle undergrowth, completely concealing it from view, and the skins would have been nearly impossible to find. Even in their present state, they were still difficult to locate. If not for the layer of flora that had grown over them, the Sentinels might not have found them at all.

Working in unison, they removed the outermost skins until they came in contact with a layer of untouched ones. Finally after sifting through the nest, they were able to choose a few unblemished skins, and Fox folded them into his pack.

Eldin smiled and took a bearing with his compass. He gestured with his hand, and they moved cautiously away from the nest in the direction of the ancient volcano.

-Chapter Seven-

Spiders

The two Sentinels wound their way silently through the jungle without further signs of trouble. They had been climbing gradually for the previous hour, and the surrounding jungle vegetation began to lessen. After a while, the ground became too steep for walking, forcing them to climb the rest of the way to the rim of the volcano.

Eldin rested on a large rock outcropping and looked out over the jungle behind them. "I think we're safely out of the hunting grounds of the lizards. Let's take a break for a moment, and I'll explain what's going to happen next."

Fox climbed out onto the escarpment and found a place to sit.

Eldin waited for him to get situated before he began. "We've passed through the jungle and collected the lizard skin, and now we only need the spider silk. If we can accomplish our next goal successfully, all that's left is backtracking through the jungle and then making it back to the coast."

Fox grinned, bobbing his head up and down. "I think we can handle that."

Eldin looked up toward the rim of the volcano. "When we get near the top, we'll need to stay quiet. Over the rim is a narrow animal trail that winds down into the mouth of the crater. The trail leads to the edge of a shallow lake where we'll probably see animal activity. The lake and the rich volcanic soil support a thriving ecosystem of exotic plants and flowers. The inhabitants of the island are irresistibly drawn to the tasty vegetation and make their way lakeside to feed."

Fox again nodded with interest, encouraging Eldin to continue.

"The cycle of life goes on, and the residents of the volcano take advantage of the situation. Gigantic spiders reside within the hollow mountain, using their webbing to snare hapless creatures that stray from the trail and wander into the many surrounding caves. Once they're snared in the webbing, there's no hope of escape."

Eldin pulled his pack off his back and set it between them. He retrieved a silver vial from one of the many pouches and carefully unscrewed the top.

Fox scrunched up his nose. "Great! I was just getting used to the rotting meat stench."

The elder Sentinel shook his head. "Don't worry… we won't need to refresh our scent until our trip back through the jungle."

He held the vial under Fox's nose and waved his hand over the opening. The bottle emitted a slight acidic odor, almost like orange rind. "What I have here is a liquid excreted from a particularly unpleasant hormonal gland on the spider. Remember when I mentioned that the spider silk is the strongest material we've ever come across? Well it's so strong that even the spiders have a difficult time extracting their prey from the webs, so they excrete a small quantity of this substance to dissolve the silk."

Fox breathed in the mild scent. "Do I even want to ask where you got that?"

"No, you don't, but don't fret. We have enough for quite some time… a little bit goes a long way. All we have to do is trickle a few drops on the webbing, and we'll be able to get what we need."

"I see," said Fox.

They picked their way over to the rim of the crater and located the trail easily enough. It wound around the interior of the crater in a gigantic spiral and came to a stop at the edge of the lake. The climate inside the crater was hot and sticky, the steep walls apparently trapping the moisture, keeping the area veiled in a perpetual mist. The stagnant air and high humidity made for such perfect growing conditions that the vegetation thrived, growing unchecked in every direction.

They had made their way down the trail about halfway when Eldin stopped next to a strange-looking rock formation. Exquisite flowering vines had grown over the area, but Eldin seemed to recognize the spot. He reached down and pushed aside a long, blossoming creeper and brushed a clump of dirt away from the rock face. There, plainly visible, was an odd-looking sigil with an arrow pointing to the perimeter wall of the crater not twenty feet to their left.

Eldin replaced the drapery of vegetation and

headed in the direction the arrow pointed. Years of growth covered the perimeter walls of the crater in a swath of thick, nearly impenetrable underbrush, hiding the rock walls from view. He withdrew a long, thin dagger from his pack and carefully sliced away some of the thicker vines, taking his time so as not to destroy the plants entirely.

When he was finished, a small opening was cleared, exposing a crack in the rock face. He slipped his knife back into his pack and removed a clear, sealed tube containing green liquid. He bent the tube with both hands until it made a distinct snapping sound but didn't break. Shortly thereafter the tube began to glow with an eerie, yellow-green light.

He held the tube into the crack and looked back at Fox. "This should be more than enough light. The tunnels stretch all through this mountain and are pocked with countless holes that let sunlight through. From what I can remember, we shouldn't have too much trouble seeing."

Fox cinched down the straps on his pack and nodded for Eldin to go ahead.

Eldin stuck his head into the tunnel. "Let's stay

quiet, keep a sharp eye out for any dangers, and by all means keep clear of the webs. The spiders can sense a disturbance in the webbing. If a creature gets snared, the vibrations of the struggling animal are transmitted down the webs, and the spider can home in on the prey."

Eldin squeezed himself into the opening and waited for Fox to follow. They were in a narrow tunnel no more than four feet wide by six feet tall. The walls were soot-stained and rough to the touch. They followed the tunnel downward at a steep slope for a short distance until it ended abruptly on a ledge that overlooked a substantial black pit. From the ledge the two Sentinels climbed down a massive sheet of flowstone that bottomed out onto a large mud-and-gravel-covered shelf. Immediately they spotted an ancient spider web extending down from the ceiling between large tree roots and natural cavern formations, but it was too far away to reach.

They followed the shelf to the edge of the pit until it fell away abruptly into blackness. They could see an opening in the wall directly across from where they were standing, but about thirty feet of open expanse separated them from the far wall.

Eldin turned to Fox and spoke in a near whisper. "There used to be a natural bridge spanning the gap. It's been years since my last visit to this cave. Something must have happened in that time."

Fox looked down into the dark abyss. "How deep does that go?"

Eldin lifted his arms and shoulders in a shrug. "Far too deep for us. I don't think anyone's ever been to the bottom and returned."

"Do we need to get into that opening in the far wall?" asked Fox.

Eldin nodded. "The passage on the other side slopes downward to a large domed room where we can find what we're here to obtain. We could turn around, but I wouldn't know which way to go from here."

"I see," said Fox. The young apprentice looked overhead and spotted a series of tree roots, but none seemed suitable for their use. "I don't see any way across other than jumping the gap, unless we're willing to turn around and look for an alternate route."

Eldin paused for a moment, taking in the situation. "You're right. I don't see any other way, myself, and I don't think we have the luxury of time to find another course."

In less than the time it took to breathe out, Fox focused his attention on the opposite wall and leapt away from the shelf. He soared through the air and landed nimbly on a narrow ledge that had been carved out beneath the passageway, more than twenty feet from where he had started. Noting that the floor sloped downward over a ditch covered with very loose gravel, the young apprentice stepped into the opening immediately. He turned around to warn Eldin, but his master was already leaping away from the ledge.

He landed on the rock ridge just in front of the passageway where Fox had been a moment before. As soon as he hit, the rock shelf groaned under his weight and started crumbling beneath his feet. Immediately the Sentinel reacted and hopped off the ledge before it crashed away into the black pit below. He leapt into the passageway, but the muddy base broke apart as soon as his feet hit the ground.

Years of water drainage had worn down the volcanic tunnel and made the passageway unstable. The physical weight of the two Sentinels had been enough to collapse the weak base into a mud-and-gravel slide that fell away down the passage. Fox and Eldin struggled against the slide, but there was simply nothing to grab. The floor gave way completely, and the two Sentinels were carried downward in the torrent of mud and loose rocks.

The tunnel opened into a vast domed cavern. The chamber was big, cylindrical, nearly ninety feet across by more than hundred feet tall. Spider webs littered the cavern from floor to ceiling, some spanning the great room from one side to the other. The roof seemed to be constructed entirely of tree roots, with holes that let thin streaks of light into the dark chamber below.

The mudslide cascaded out of the tunnel onto a narrow ledge and plummeted into a dark pool of water that formed the bottom of the cavern, fifty feet below. Swept downward by the slide, the two Sentinels exploded out of the passage.

Eldin had been clawing at the walls of the cavern to stop from falling over the edge but could find nothing to grab hold of. He exited first and fell through the air for about twenty feet before tumbling into a huge web that spanned the length of the room.

Fox followed his master but had managed to pull a dagger from his belt before being thrown out of the tunnel. As the ground beneath him began dropping away over the precipice, he was compelled to thrust the dagger through the loose gravel in an attempt to arrest his speed. Just as his feet slid over the edge, he pressed downward with all his might, encasing the dagger up to its hilt in the rock wall of the tunnel. The instant it held, he reached out with his free hand and jammed his fingers through the volcanic gravel until they latched onto something solid. The flood of rock and gravel cascaded over his head, pouring mud and silt into his clothing and nearly forcing him to loose his grip on the dagger and the wall, but somehow he managed to hold on.

After a few harrowing moments, the slide finally subsided, and Fox was able to drag himself clear of the rubble and onto a narrow rock shelf away from the debris. He pulled his dagger from the wall, unconsciously wiped the blade clean, and inserted it back into his belt. There was enough light shining through the holes in the ceiling so that he could get a fairly good idea of his surroundings, and he stepped cautiously to the edge of the rock ledge, peering down into the belly of the cavern.

He spotted Eldin straight away, entangled at the very edge of the largest spider web he had ever seen. His master was struggling in the webbing but was apparently no worse for wear. The problem was that he was upside down, hanging from the sticky snare by his feet. Assuming that the webbing was as strong as Eldin had proclaimed, Fox had no fear of his teacher falling… but how was he going to get him out of there?

Far above their heads deep within the shadows of her lair, the spider could feel her web humming. She reached out with one of her forelegs and gently pressed the claw onto the vibrating web.

Yes, it feels as though the tunnels have brought me a little meal!

She climbed away from her nest and attached a single web line to the roof of the cavern, then silently began to lower herself to the waiting victim.

Fox was trying to figure out what he needed to

do when he felt a cold chill run down his spine. He looked down at Eldin, who was starring at something far over his head. Slowly Fox turned and looked upward to the roof of the cavern. There he spotted the biggest, fiercest-looking spider he could possibly have imagined.

The spider was a good distance overhead, but even in the dim light Fox could discern her general appearance. She had a large brown body covered in bristling hairs, with red and black bands of color over her abdomen and legs. Eight closely grouped pairs of eyes, arranged in three vertical sets on each side of her head and two in the middle, watched every move that both he and Eldin made.

Fortunately for the elves, she was taking plenty of time to get down to their level, which gave Fox a chance to think. The young apprentice took in the details of the entire room, and ignoring their previous pact of silence, yelled down to Eldin.

"Can you get to the vial containing the web liquid?"

Eldin nodded and carefully removed his pack from his back. Cautiously he flipped it right-side-up so that the contents would not spill out when he opened the flap. He reached inside and withdrew the vial, waited for his apprentice to signal, and tossed the small silver container up to Fox's waiting hands.

Fox reached out and snatched the vial from midair. He withdrew his sword from its sheath and laid it on the ground in front of him. He looked for the spider and discovered that she was getting uncomfortably close. Hurriedly he unscrewed the cap of the vial and dribbled a few drops of the enzyme on the blade. He was relieved to see that the substance didn't seem to harm the metal in any way but was also nervous, aware that his grand scheme might not work.

He looked up again to see two large mandibles snapping open and shut above his head, their fangs dripping green venom into the black pit below. Involuntarily he moved closer to the wall of the cavern, even though the direction of the creature's descent would take her well away from the ledge on which he stood, on her way toward Eldin.

The spider began to descend through the cavern on a long line, inching ever closer to her intended next meal. The prey was entangled in her web below, hanging there helplessly and awaiting the inevitable. Then she spotted Fox.

There was an intruder in her lair. Fox was crouched against the cavern wall, fearful to move. Slowly she dropped down to his level and examined this trespasser with all eight of her eyes. He didn't move, only stared back at her, waiting to see what would happen next.

The spider apparently realized then that this little creature wasn't afraid of her, and that seemed to worry her in turn. Out of fear she struck out with her front foreleg, her claw tearing into the volcanic wall just over Fox's head. He ducked out of the way quickly but didn't make any threatening moves in retaliation. The spider hissed and snapped her jaws at him, but he didn't fight back.

Fox waited breathlessly as the spider lashed out at him. Fearing that retaliation might force him to kill her, he decided to play a dangerous game in the hope that his lack of action would stop the spider from making an all-out assault. Moments passed as they starred each other down, but in the end his gambled paid off, and she left him alone.

The spider could have leapt away from her web line and attacked him on the ledge, but perhaps something told her that this little beast might have a sting of his own. She decided to ignore him for the moment and deal with the prey trapped below. He watched as she descended down her line, moving ever closer to Eldin. His teacher wasn't stirring, but Fox could see that he was ready to fight if need be. Sword in hand, the young apprentice steadied himself at the edge of the rock ledge, studying the room and waiting until the spider was only inches from Eldin's head.

Long ago the cavern had been filled with numerous naturally formed rock bridges. At one time they had spanned the room from one end to the other. Years of erosion had left only the ruins, crumbled and broken into heaps of shattered rock on the cavern floor far below. The young Sentinel looked at these crumbling formations and knew exactly what to do.

At the last moment, Fox leaped away from the shelf, flying into the air and slashing out with his enzyme-coated sword. The blade cut into the thin web-line that was easily supporting the weight of the eight-legged monstrosity. For an instant the web-line had offered resistance, but the enzyme on the sword had worked and allowed his weapon to slice through the material.

Fox landed slightly off balance on the edge of a rock escarpment that had once been the supporting structure of a natural bridge. The rock grumbled under him, and small chunks of debris fell away, but the structure seemed to hold his weight. He turned and watched as the surprised spider tumbled away from Eldin, her own weight and momentum preventing her from catching hold of the web in which Eldin was trapped. She fell into the darkness, and with a tremendous splash she hit the muddy water of an underground pool far below.

Apparently Eldin's glow-stick had fallen away during the slide and was now floating in the water far below, illuminating the muddy lake with an eerie green glow. The stick emitted minimal light, but it was enough for him to see that he hadn't killed the beast. She was struggling in the dark water, extremely annoyed at what had just transpired. So angry that it wouldn't be long before she recovered enough to swim to the cavern wall, possibly spin a new line of webbing, and climb back up to their level.

The boy quickly dribbled a few more drops of the precious enzyme on his sword and removed a rope from his backpack. He tied the vial to one of the free ends of the rope and lowered it down to Eldin. He then secured the other end of the rope to the rock structure and wrapped the center section around his own waist for extra support.

Fox peered over the edge of the rock formation and watched Eldin untie the vial and secure the end of the rope around his waist. Fox took advantage of that time by hacking away at large piece of webbing that was secured not far from where he was standing. He had removed the web and just finished packing it into his backpack when he felt the rope go taunt. He braced himself against the pull of the rope and assisted Eldin as he climbed hand over hand up to the escarpment.

Just as Eldin pulled himself over the edge of the rock, they spotted the spider climbing up the wall about thirty feet away from them. She turned to watch them for a moment before scuttling farther up the wall until she reached another web just over their heads. She then threw herself away from the rock wall, soared through the air, and grasped hold of the webbing. She dangled for a split second at the edge, then heaved herself under the expanse so that she was hanging upside down on the bottom of the giant web. She hesitated for an instant to gain better footing, then quickly began to crawl toward the two Sentinels.

Fox slashed with his sword, cutting through the remaining strands of spider web attached to Eldin's legs. "I think we best get moving," he suggested.

Eldin turned and watched as the massive creature crawled ever closer to them, venom dripping from her fangs and sizzling on the rock formations below. "I think that's a good idea."

Fox quickly stuffed the rope into his pack and slid his sword into its sheath as they examined the room for the easiest way out. They spotted a partially intact bridge and leapt away from the rock outcropping as the spider lashed out with her forelegs from only a few feet away. The two Sentinels landed on a narrow arch that immediately began to collapse under their weight. Reacting instantly, they jumped from the collapsing archway and leaped upward, grabbing hold of a sturdier expanse that still spanned most of the room. It held for the moment, and they threw themselves up onto the rock ledge.

The spider hissed at them from below and ran to the edge of the web so that she could climb back up. She then scurried up the wall and jumped from web to web, unwilling to let the two elves get away so easily.

They ran to the end of the bridge and spied a narrow opening in the roof of the cavern, about twenty feet over their heads. They stepped into a narrow shaft of light, which blinded them for an instant. The spider took advantage of their disorientation and landed with a thud on the rock bridge, then chased them to the cavern wall.

Trapped between the spider and their escape, the two Sentinels stood motionless. The arachnid reared back on her hind legs and threw herself forward, spitting venom at the two trespassers in the process. In unison Fox and Eldin dodged the toxin and watched as it splattered harmlessly on the wall behind them. Eldin leaped into the air and grabbed a large tree root that extended down from the ceiling. He reached hand over hand until he was just under the opening.

Fox dodged another series of attacks from the

spider but was quickly running out of options. Eldin pulled himself out of the opening and yelled down for Fox to follow. The spider slashed out with her front forelegs and tore gashes into the volcanic wall where the apprentice had been a moment before. The young elf jumped up and grabbed one of the tree roots that had broken through the ceiling of the cavern, and continuing to grasp these one by one, he swung himself across the ceiling and out the narrow hole to his waiting teacher.

-Chapter Eight-

Black Dragon

It was dark by the time the two Sentinels reached the coast. Their return down the volcano and through the jungle had gone without incident, but by now they were ready for a quiet evening.

Fox dropped his pack in the sand next to a fallen palm tree about halfway between the jungle and the water. "Should we call the birds?"

Eldin nodded without speaking. Then he dumped his pack next to his apprentice and wandered away down the coast. He had remained quiet during their descent from the volcano and subsequently through the jungle, and Fox was concerned that he might have made a mistake during their journey. His teacher's lack of conversation only heightened the young apprentice's apprehension.

Fox pulled a small, thin whistle from his pack and blew into it. No audible sound emitted from the little device, but the young elf seemed satisfied. A few moments later, he spotted two specks on the horizon, and he knew that the birds had heeded his call. He unpacked the rest of his gear and sat himself down on the log. Soon after, the birds landed not far away in a cloud of sand, and Fox immediately began to remove the saddles and riding gear from their backs.

By the time Eldin returned from his walk, Fox had a makeshift camp set up and a small fire burning. He passed Eldin a bowl of warm soup and smiled. "Is everything okay? Have I done something wrong?"

Eldin accepted the bowl with a sincere thank you and shook his head. "Fox, I've been so concerned about *my* performance that it didn't even occur to me that you would misinterpret my mood. You did nothing wrong. As a matter of fact, if it weren't for your quick thinking, I would have been forced into a fight."

Fox looked over at his teacher for a moment. It had never crossed his mind that Eldin might be the one who had done something wrong. Since the incident in the cave, Fox had been concerned that he should have alerted Eldin to the loose rocks before he made the jump over the gap. "I was worried that I didn't warn you quickly enough about the loose flooring, but you jumped just as I had realized that our combined weight would cause the slide."

Eldin nodded. "It was me. I acted in haste, without thinking. I should have let you go ahead and scout out the passageway before joining you. In my haste to return to Greylok, I put us both in jeopardy."

He hesitated for a minute, then went on. "You have passed all of your tests with flying colors. I will recommend immediate promotion and hope you will accept my apology for jeopardizing the mission."

Fox shook his head. "Thank you, and absolutely no apologies are necessary." He could have said more, but he felt that Eldin was truly bothered by his own personal demons at that moment, so he decided not to pursue the matter.

By morning Fox and Eldin were on wing again, flying through the early morning hours en route to Halfway Island. The day went by easily enough, and by early that evening they had spotted the island, landed, and made camp in the same general location where they had camped a couple of days earlier. It was a clear, pleasant evening, and the two Sentinels quickly fell asleep under the stars.

The night passed without incident, and by the sixth day of their journey they were once again flying on their way to the coast. By daybreak the island was behind them, and ahead lay an endless stretch of ocean. Their intent was to reach the coast by midday, take a short respite, and complete the final leg to the edge of the Great Forest by dusk.

By midmorning a fierce storm had blown in, bringing with it heavy rains and strong winds. They battled through the torrential downpour, hunkering down within their protective riding gear, and rode out the maelstrom. Periodic checks of their compasses indicated that they were on course for the coast, but they could feel the great birds struggling against the powerful winds.

It was still early in the afternoon when they broke free of the front and were within sight of the coastline. A jagged, rocky cliff fronted by a thin ribbon of sandy beach loomed ahead of them, and immediately Fox knew that something was wrong. The storm had blown them a good distance to the north and considerably off track. Their birds had been able to maintain the correct heading through the storm, but they could not control the direction the winds blew them.

Eldin brought the birds in low and landed them on a thin strip of sand within the shadow of the towering cliffs. He removed his map from his flight pack and studied it while Fox tended to the birds.

"It looks like we've been blown about two hours north of where we should be," said Eldin. "We'll need to fly in a southwesterly direction to get back on track. The problem is that it keeps us over the swamp for longer than I would like to be there."

Fox positioned a bowl of fresh water for Stormwise and took the map from Eldin. He studied the drawing for a few moments and agreed with a grunt, the memory of the hideous Manx still fresh in his mind.

The young apprentice traced the distance with his fingers and looked up at the cliffs. "I don't think we should rest here for long, though. As I recall from our last visit, these cliffs harbor a less-than-delightful assortment of dangerous predators."

Eldin followed his eye to the jagged cliffs above. "Quite right. Let's give the birds a quick drink and mount up. If we hurry we should be able to clear the swamp before nightfall. Frankly, the last place I want to be when the sun goes down is over that horrific bog."

While the birds drank, they checked their gear and made final preparations to leave. After a quick inspection of the area, they pulled themselves into their saddles and urged their steeds to a takeoff.

With tremendous downward strokes of their wings, the raptors leapt away from the ground and accelerated into the air. It wasn't long before the ominous cliffs were left far behind, and only the vast, murky green swath of the Swamp of Doom and Despair lay ahead.

Drago had made his residence in the marsh long ago. He resided in an underground cavern deep beneath the black waters, directly below the spot where he now lurked. Waiting for his lunch, he allowed just the crest of his head to break the surface of the still, dark waters that surrounded him.

Drago was a massive black dragon and one of the eldest of his kind. His actual age had long been forgotten, but few forgot that he existed. Tales of his temper preceded him. As he had grown more ancient, he'd become ever more malevolent, until now he was interested only in filling his stomach and increasing the size of his treasure horde.

The shadows began to grow long, and Drago's stomach growled. He rotated his head from side to side, creating a rippling effect that extended across the still waters. Drago adored the swamp, with its foul waters and the evil denizens that resided within its borders. They were his kind--sinister and cruel.

It was getting late in the day, and his stomach was continuing to growl. Through the ages the huge dragon had learned to use the swamp to suit his own needs and often found himself listening intently to the sound vibrations that were carried across the surface of the black lake. He found that if he positioned his head just above the still waters of the marsh, he could use it as a natural amplifier and heighten his own keen senses to detect an intruder--or a lunch, in this case--miles away.

The two Sentinels soon grew weary. They had

long been flying through a layer of thin haze that adhered to the trees and dampened their spirits. They were cruising a few feet above the treetops, relying on the instincts of their birds to keep them from colliding with any unseen branches.

When they finally broke through the dense layer of fog, they felt almost relieved to find themselves crossing over a black bog that stretched away as far as they could see. The still waters below them had grown so thick with slime and floating vegetation that the water itself was hardly visible. Mile after mile the bog continued, broken only by an occasional island or the movement of a creature hidden in its murky depths.

Both Sentinels felt uneasy so close to the large expanse of foul water below, but neither rider wished to waste more time by steering around the bog. Their fears subsided when the far shore came into view and the slime-coated waters gradually changed to a black, mirror-like surface. At the shoreline they spotted a cluster of hardy cypress trees protruding from the bog; but just as the birds neared the beach, they flew back into another layer of dense fog and lost what few bearings they'd had.

Drago smiled, and the foul waters of the bog rushed into his gaping mouth. He titled his head forward and arched his long neck so that his spinal crest broke through the surface of the water. The cool, wet air condensed and dripped down the translucent membrane of the crest, and his hypersensitive skin absorbed the slightest vibrations in the air. He laid his neck back into the water and lifted his massive head high enough to see across the lake. He gazed deep into the misty sky, snuffling at the air and listening to the bog. Satisfied, he dropped his skull-like head back into the water so that only his eyes and a small portion of his crest broke the perfectly still surface… and then he waited.

The two riders urged their mounts to rise out of the ever-present fog so that they could search once again for the boundary of the swamp. Suddenly they both sensed imminent danger from below, and they heaved their birds to either side of the perceived threat. An instant later an immense dragon exploded from the fog bank and forced itself between the two riders. In a wave of force, it ripped between them, tearing at the air with its deadly claws and ramming its massive, leathery wings into both Morwen and Stormwise. Before they had a chance to recover, the beast twisted around in the air and dove back into the fray, snapping at the birds with its gaping jaws.

Stormwise recovered first, and her quick predatory reflexes allowed her to steer away, barely avoiding the next attack. Morwen, however, was not fast enough. The larger of the two birds, he was not as agile as the falcon. The dragon collided with him at full force. Its claws slashed into the great bird's wings, tearing away huge sections of bloodied feathers, breaking bones and forcing the hawk to fall from the sky.

Eldin held onto his saddle for dear life as Morwen struggled to stay aloft, but the bird's wings had been savagely broken, and he couldn't regain control. They plummeted into the dense fog, keenly aware that the ground was quickly approaching. With nothing left to try, Eldin urged his bird to pull his ragged wings tightly to his sides, just as they crashed into the dense canopy of the swamp.

Fox watched helplessly from above, realizing

that he would be next if he didn't take action. He turned Stormwise back around to locate the dragon but couldn't spot it in the fog. The dragon was well aware of him, however, and skimmed silently over the treetops under cover of a thin layer of mist. Flexing its massive muscles in preparation for the next move, it turned its head upward and watched its prey far above.

Then suddenly the dragon dove downward, accelerating as it descended to only inches above the treetops before turning upward again and flying straight up into the sky. The dragon whipped in front of the elf and his steed, its armor-coated muscles rippling under the extreme strain of the maneuver and trembling as if they might give out entirely. Finally, after climbing hundreds of feet into the sky, it gave in to gravity and rolled onto its back before dipping its head toward the ground in order to complete the giant loop. The trick had worked, and the dragon was now in the perfect position to dive straight at Stormwise.

For only an instant, Fox admired the beauty of the maneuver, but quickly regained his composure and pulled in the reins of his harness, forcing his bird to avoid the attacking beast. It was coming at them incredibly fast, trying to ram the falcon with its two forward-pointing horns. At that speed, Fox knew a hit would sheer both bird and rider cleanly in two.

Miraculously they managed to avoid the strike, and the dragon raced past them with blinding speed. Eons of fighting aerial battles had obviously left the ancient reptile with a few more tricks up it sleeve. As it swept past Stormwise, it lashed out with its tail, smashing into both raptor and elf.

Fox had thought they might avoid the assault when he first saw the dragon sweep by, but in that same instant he realized his shortsightedness. The tail of the beast had slammed into Stormwise's back, missing Fox by mere inches. Stormwise collapsed under the pressure of the blow and fell from the sky, out of control.

Fox grabbed hold of his saddle and pressed himself flat against the back of his mount. An instant later they crashed into the dense canopy of the swamp. Branches and sticks lashed the young elf, tearing into his face and back. Stormwise tried in vain to soften the landing by extending her muscular legs to break the fall, but she was simply moving too fast for that to do any good.

They dropped through the canopy and impacted with the ground in a violent spray of mud and water, which threw Fox from the saddle and hurtled him through the air. He hit the ground hard but managed to force himself into a ball and roll out of the fall, displacing much of the impact across his entire body. He tumbled away from Stormwise until the energy of the fall was dissipated. Then he sprang to his feet at the last instant so that he could survey the situation quickly. The rolling fall and the soft earth had prevented serious injury, but he still had the dragon to contend with.

He spotted the beast circling overhead. His mind raced, and he scanned the area for signs of Morwen and his master. He ran over to check on Stormwise and found her to be unconscious, but her breathing was steady. She looked hurt, but not in critical condition. Fox gave her a quick once-over but knew there was nothing he could really do until the dragon was dealt with. He glanced up and saw that the dragon had stopped circling and was heading toward the spot where Morwen had likely crashed. Fox stroked Stormwise's head for a moment and murmured encouragement, even though she wasn't yet awake.

"I'll be back as soon as I can," he assured her.

Then he took off at a dead run in the direction where Morwen, Eldin, and the dragon would be found.

fb
©2006

-Chapter Nine-

Drago

Fox found Eldin knee-deep in mud between the shore of the marsh and a thicket of dense trees. Morwen was tangled in a mass of thick vines and struggling to pull free. His right wing was a mess and hanging at an unnatural angle. To make matters worse, he was trapped in the mud, and his thrashing about was only aggravating the situation.

By working together, the two Sentinels were able to free the struggling bird and keep him from sinking farther into the bog. When they finally separated him from the vines, they found that his wing wasn't as bad as they'd first thought--but he wasn't going to fly anytime soon, and his squawking and yelping was beginning to draw unwanted attention.

They had just begun to tend to the wing when they sensed a disturbance of the air behind them. The two Sentinels tensed and turned to face the marsh. Even

Morwen stopped squawking as the black dragon landed in a clearing not fifty yards away.

The dragon's head resembled a skull with a layer of dark flesh pulled tight over the bone, accentuating deep eye sockets and a wide, flat nasal opening. It had two huge, forward-curving horns and a translucent gray crest that peaked just behind the head and tapered off at the base of the neck. A deep black at the chest gradually faded into dark gray toward the edges of its mottled wings. The beast smelled like the swamp, and when it moved they could see that its coloring was a perfect camouflage in the bleak surroundings.

Fox and Eldin drew their swords and slowly stepped out of the mud onto firmer ground. Two malevolent, pupil-less eyes stared them down, glowing a dark, swampy green in the dim light. Noxious green smoke curled upward from its nostrils, and it grinned at its chosen prey, exposing row after row of dagger-like teeth.

The dragon reared its neck and lifted its head to the sky. Eldin glanced at Fox, and they both dove into the nearby brush, taking cover behind a cluster of ancient cypress trees.

The beast thrust forward its serpentine head, opened its mouth, and curled its thin black lips back from a splotched pink gum line. A cone-shaped spray of acid erupted from its open maw, spreading outward in a swath of destruction and melting everything that stood in its way.

The two Sentinels ducked low behind the trees as the acid sizzled and burned all around them. Splatter from the blast burned holes through their clothes and blistered their skin, but the trees protected them from serious injury. When it was over, they surveyed the damage and knew that this wasn't going to be an easy fight--it would be a battle for their lives.

Eldin slipped from behind the cover of trees and charged at the dragon. He moved so quickly that the creature hardly saw him coming at first. The Sentinel slashed outward with his sword, striking at the soft flesh near the beast's nose, but the dragon reacted to the attack instinctively and blocked the sword with one of his curved horns. They battled back and forth, each countering the other's attacks while gauging each other's skill. Then Eldin pivoted and dropped to one knee, effectively reversing his strike. He allowed his blade to dip toward the ground before he wheeled himself around and swung it upward in a great arc, making contact with the dragon's horn in a devastating blow. The keen elven blade slashed the horn, cleaving it from the beast's head.

The dragon reared up on its hind legs in fury, roaring a protest to the heavens. Fox took advantage of the opportunity and rushed from the trees, lashing out with his own sword. He stopped only inches from the dragon's belly and twisted his body as much as he could. A moment later he thrust himself around again, causing his riding cloak to fan outward from the spin. At the same time, he lashed out with his sword, striking the dragon across the belly in a great slash that should have gutted the beast in one blow. But even his elven blade wasn't enough to slice through the dragon's scaly armor-plating. The beast yelped in pain, but its thick skin prevented the blow from proving mortal and only served to antagonize the dragon further.

Fox rallied and dashed over to Eldin's side. "A strike like that should have torn him open, shouldn't it? This beast must really be old... truly ancient and powerful."

"Yes. Our strategy was sound. We should have defeated it with that combination, but all we achieved was to make it angrier."

The dragon dropped to the ground and thrust its remaining horn at Fox. The apprentice dodged the blow, only to find himself directly in the path of the beast's razor claws. Instinctively he ducked and rolled away from the attack, but not before suffering a wicked gash across his back from one of the talons.

Eldin redoubled his efforts to draw the beast away from Fox and give the younger elf a chance to recover. He swung at the beast time and again, striking and slashing, whirling and spinning, cutting deep into the dragon's thick hide but hardly inflicting anything more than superficial damage to the huge beast.

In a running jump, Fox leapt onto the dragon's flank and hopped up onto its back. He hacked away at its neck and shoulders, tearing holes and gashes through the sensitive spinal crest. The dragon shuddered in agony, twisting and gyrating its body to shake the boy loose, but Fox held on and wouldn't be shaken. Slipping the blade between the loose armor plates on the back of the dragon's neck, he plunged his sword to its hilt.

The dragon roared in pain and thrashed its body round and round, kicking up a maelstrom of flying dirt and debris. It lashed out with its tail, slapping it back and fourth between the shore and the bog and throwing mud in every direction. In rage it slammed into a nearby thicket of trees, smashing them with such force that it tore them from the ground and tossed them through the air like a child's toys.

The dragon's muscles rippled under the armor plating as it heaved itself back and fourth, causing the ground to tremble in its wake. Fox couldn't hang on any longer, and he grabbed the handle of his sword and pulled it out just as he was flung from the dragon's back.

Eldin had barely enough time to watch Fox hit the ground and roll to his feet before the dragon turned on them again. The beast went wild, attacking with a renewed wrath. It lashed out with its claws and snapped at them with its vice-like jaws in a frenzy of rage. Eldin blocked as many blows as he could, but the unabated fury prevented him from getting very close.

Fox joined the attack, and the battle raged on, each opponent dishing out blow after blow. The Sentinels whirled and spun, thrusting with their swords and slicing away at the dragon, their motions blending smoothly from one attack to the next. They twisted and turned, pivoting away from each attack and drawing each strike away into nothing, but the dragon wouldn't tire. It fought on, slashing with its claws and forcing the two elves to break away from the fight repeatedly to avoid blows that could easily sever them in two.

The battle wore on, and they were all tiring from the constant exertion and loss of blood from numerous wounds. Fox tried valiantly once again to leap on the dragon's back, as this seemed to be its only vulnerable spot. In response, the dragon spread wide its massive wings and flapped them, sending downward a current of air that kept the Sentinels firmly on the ground. In retaliation they plunged their weapons into the creature's leathery wings, tearing and ripping the thin skin until it was nothing more than shreds.

The dragon reared back on its hind legs. Then it pivoted and lashed out with its mighty tail in an attempt to club them down. In unison the Sentinels leaped over the swinging tail, but the dragon had anticipated their evasion, and it bounded into the air with its powerful hind legs. Instinctively it spread wide its shredded wings, but they were now useless. Flight wasn't what the creature had in mind now, however. In a rumbling roar that permeated the air for miles, it uttered incomprehensible words in an ancient language.

The Sentinels guessed the consequences, but there was nothing they could do. The dragon slammed into the ground, compressing its legs on impact and forcing a shockwave of magical energy to flow into the earth. The ground rippled with static electricity and exploded in an expanding blast that shook the ground. It created a wave of dirt and mud that radiated outward from the creature like water splashing from a pool when struck by a heavy stone.

The force of the quake walloped the Sentinels before they had a chance to react, rattling them to the bone and knocking the air from their lungs. They both fell to the ground, gasping for breath, and the dragon knew it had the upper hand. The beast gathered its remaining strength and raised a clawed hand. It spread wide its talons and released a final surge of energy that crackled through the air.

The two Sentinels tried to roll out of the way, but the dragon anticipated the move and turned its strike directly onto Eldin. Static electricity pulsed and crackled in a smoking ring on Eldin's chest where the magical lightning had struck him. The dragon hissed in satisfaction and heaved its massive body forward to crush the fallen Sentinel with one final blow.

Fox saw the beast coming and leapt to his feet, mustering what strength he had left to position himself between Eldin and the giant black serpent. The dragon spotted him and stopped in its tracks to swing its tail around like a whip and strike at the weakened apprentice. The young elf was simply too exhausted to react in time, and the tail struck him cleanly across his chest. The force of the blow crushed his ribs and lifted him from the ground, tossing him backwards through the air and into a distant scrub oak.

Fox slammed into the tree, and the back of his head met the unforgiving wood, which knocked him unconscious. The last thing he was aware of was sliding down the trunk with his head slumped into his chest.

Fox's distraction had worked to give Eldin the

time he needed to crawl out of the way. The dragon recovered quickly and reoriented itself, but its next strike missed the mark, and it only managed to tear gouges in the mud where the Sentinel had been a moment before.

The dragon measured and then savored the situation, realizing that it had the upper hand. It followed after the crawling Sentinel and stepped in front of him, but Eldin had one more trick up his sleeve. He stopped in his tracks, allowing the beast to straddle him with its massive claws.

The dragon looked down at the fallen elf and hissed in his face with its feted breath. Eldin knew he could be crushed at any moment, but instead of panicking he reached down within himself and mustered all his residual strength. He grasped the handle of his sword with both hands and pulled himself into a crouching position. Before the dragon had time to react, the Sentinel thrust himself and his sword upward, exerting every last ounce of his remaining power. He stabbed the blade into the dragon's neck, next to the jawbone, where the armor was soft and vulnerable. He pushed the sword to its hilt, forcing both his energy and all his will into the attack.

Eldin fell back and away from the dragon and collapsed to the ground, spent. His body was broken, his strength completely consumed, and he needed time to recover, if any could be found.

Drago reared in agony. The blade had torn his throat and severed vital arteries. The wound was mortal, and the great dragon knew he was going to die. He fell to the ground, shaking the earth beneath him. With the last of his strength, he cast one final spell and willed his very being to leave the dying physical body.

Drago was an ancient black dragon--nearly the oldest of his kind--and his magic was great. He wasn't ready to depart this world just yet, and he had the power to keep his soul locked into the mortal world. He wound the spell together in his mind and uttered the final words to place it into being.

In the next moment, the beast's head slammed into the ground, and the light drained from the murky green eyes. A stream of inky smoke curled up and away from the dragon's nostrils, taking shape a few feet above the ground. It formed a vaporous trail, itself vaguely resembling a winged dragon. Then it drifted through the air for a few moments, leaving a faint trace of fog in its passing.

Drago's black soul found Eldin collapsed on the ground and hovered inches above his unconscious form. Lazily it drifted over the Sentinel, lightly grazing his body with its vaporous wings. Satisfied, it drifted to the elf's face and waited for him to breathe in. The dark soul of Drago, the black dragon, positioned itself over Eldin's mouth, inches from his lips, waiting to be inhaled with his next breath.

Eldin's unconscious mind recognized the intrusion immediately but was helpless to resist. His energy was gone, and the spirit of the dragon was far too strong for him to fight. In his last independent moments, he snatched what memories he could and hid himself from the trespasser, stealing away into deep, nearly forgotten corridors of his mind that the beast could likely never find--locking away his own soul until he could safely break free.

Eldin's eyes sprang open, glowing an eerie green. His body was weak, but the dragon magic was already beginning to work. His wounds started to heal;

the bruises and cuts that covered his body began to knit themselves back together and to fade as his strength returned. His silver-streaked hair shifted through various shades of gray and gradually darkened until it reverted to a uniform shiny black.

The elder Sentinel stood upright, stretching his body and lifting his hands to the sky, feeling new muscle forming and rippling under his torn clothes. The dragon magic was washing away years, strengthening his body and healing his wounds, returning the elf to his prime.

Soon Drago awakened fully inside the living body of the Sentinel, and the green glow faded from his elven eyes. Drago reached deep into Eldin's mind, probing it for bits and pieces of useful information. He had access to everything, instantly absorbing what the senior Sentinel knew.

A smile crossed his lips and his eyes glowed bright green once more.

He knows of the Wyrd... and the location of the key.

-Chapter Ten-

Escape

Now upright in Eldin's revived elf body, Drago grabbed the handle of the sword and pulled it from his old dragon carcass. He heard Morwen making a racket and turned and spotted the hawk struggling in the mud a short distance away.

Drago approached the bird, smiling and pretending to be his friend, but Morwen would have none of it. He took one look at the imposter and knew immediately that this was not his master. The giant hawk squawked and hissed at the being in Eldin's body, warning him not to get too close.

Drago's smile turned to a snarl, and he lifted his hand, palm outward in a gesture of caution. A small circle of yellow light ignited in the center of his palm and gradually intensified to a more concentrated glow. He pressed outward with his hand, and energy coursed from his palm, striking Morwen directly in the face. The energy crackled around the bird, instantly knocking him unconscious.

Drago placed his hand over the raptor's beak and felt a gentle breath of air emanating from the insensible creature. *Well, isn't that interesting...?* he thought. *That should have killed the bird. I suppose the fight and the healing of this body must have weakened me more than I thought.*

He spied the saddle and riding gear still strapped to the hawk, and one corner of his lips curved upward. *Well, then... I think I'm going to pay a visit to an old friend in the mountains. The trip should give me a little more time to heal before I concentrate my efforts on the Wyrd.*

With little effort Drago removed the saddle and gear from the hawk and carried it to a nearby clearing before dumping it to the ground. He looked into the sky and sniffed at the breeze. He cupped his hands around his mouth and turned to face the marsh before calling into the air. His voice raised in pitch as he trilled a magical melody that fused with the wind. The magic drifted through the marsh, echoing through the trees and over the dark, muddy waters. Now slightly winded, he sat on a rotted log and waited for a response.

He didn't have to wait long before a dark speck appeared on the horizon. The little brown dragon winged its way over the marsh, responding to the call without question. The ancient black's call was too strong to resist. The voice may have sounded different--strange and not dragon-like--but he didn't dare question the magic of the Old One.

The little brown was the first to arrive, but others were close behind. Within moments, twenty or more dragons filled the sky above Drago. They circled the clearing, making long, lazy turns above the marsh but a bit too fearful to land. He stood and watched the dragons gliding for a moment, examining each of them carefully from the ground.

Greens, browns, and grays filled the sky; a good assortment had heeded his call. He watched all of them carefully before making a decision. Finally he pointed to a large green and called it to him with the strange, magical voice dragons use among themselves.

The beast landed a short distance away, giving

the carcass of the ancient black a wide berth. Drago approached the creature and examined it from head to tail before he was satisfied enough to dismiss the others. He waved his hand in the air, and the remaining dragons dispersed back into the swamp.

The dragon he had chosen was a good size, with a dark, mottled green and traces of gray across its chest and wings. It had a large, reptilian head, with two swept-back horns protruding from either side of a short spinal crest that tapered down its neck. The creature was slightly larger than the hawk Eldin had ridden, but not too big to keep under control.

Drago stroked his hand across a series of tiny hornlets that jutted out from the beast's lower jaw. He examined the dragon's eyes and noted that the pupils were like large, feline slits, each surrounded with a field of red. This indicated that the creature was still quite young, as far as dragons went--a more mature dragon would have lost the pupil almost entirely--but it would still suit his needs perfectly.

He grabbed the dragon by the ear, pulling hard on the thin membrane until he got its full attention. The beast hissed but made no attempt to pull away. Drago knew what the beast was thinking: How could this little human body that stank of civilization contain the soul of the ancient black dragon that lay dead at the edge of the bog?

Drago whispered into the green dragon's ear, weaving magic into his voice so that he could influence the young beast as he wished. The green absorbed the magic like a sponge, as Drago's words seeped into the weak-minded creature's mind and brought it completely under his control.

Utterly under Drago's spell, the green dragon dropped to its knees and patiently allowed the transformed Sentinel to put Morwen's saddle on his back. It hardly flinched as he adjusted the gear and returned the elven sword to its sheath. He cinched down the harness lines and climbed onto the dragon's back. The green dragon reared and struggled for a moment under the elf's weight, but Drago pressed his magical will into his voice and steadied its mind.

He took one quick look around the swamp before forcing the beast into the air once more. The dragon climbed into the sky, using the late afternoon thermals to help it soar above the tree line. Drago pulled in the reins and pointed the dragon northward, effortlessly guiding the creature over the marsh.

Yes... I think I'm going to visit my dear old friends in the mountains. I'm sure they'll be pleased to see me.

Hour's later Fox woke with a throbbing headache. He reached up his hand and winced from the pain as he discovered the huge knot on the back of his head. His whole body ached from countless lacerations. Most of the wounds had stopped bleeding, but he knew he wasn't out of trouble. His mind raced to Eldin, and he wondered what had happened to his fallen teacher.

He tried to stand but fell back in agony, dizzy from the pain. His chest ached from more than just superficial cuts and bruises; the dragon's tail had done some serious damage. He felt his ribcage, and a wave of white-hot pain raced through him. He had at least two broken ribs, maybe more.

The young Sentinel slowed his breathing and relied on his years of training to block some of the pain from his mind. He felt around blindly for his sword and was pleased that he somehow hadn't managed to lose it.

He reached into the tall grass, and his fingers tightened around the grip. He grabbed the handle tight and gently wedged the blade into the ground. Using the sword as a prop, he slowly rose to his feet. Dizzy from the intense pain of the effort, he steadied himself against a tree.

The young elf took a shallow breath. Yes, his ribs were broken, his whole body ached, and he might have a concussion, but he wasn't going to let that stop him. He knew that if he could stand, he could still walk, and that was exactly what he did next. Gently he took one step forward, followed by another and another, until he found himself standing a few feet from the fallen black dragon.

It was very late in the day, and soon the light would be gone. In vain he searched the area for Eldin, but he didn't sense his master's presence, and he knew he wouldn't soon find the elder Sentinel. In the fading light, he could find no trace of his teacher. He tried to yell, but his broken ribs prevented much more than a whisper escaping his lips.

Fox found Morwen still trapped in the mud, alive but unconscious. He made the bird as comfortable as possible, certain that there was nothing more he could do for him while he was still out cold. The bird's saddle was missing, and this disturbed the young Sentinel, intensifying his concern for what might have happened to Eldin. Then his thoughts turned to Stormwise, and he headed off toward the location where he had left his mount hours before.

He found her in the same spot. When he arrived, she was awake but in a very poor mood. She squawked in protest and snapped at the air, but Fox knew that her bark was far worse than her bite. She wanted him to know that he should never have left her stuck and alone for so long. The elf slowly approached the bird, giving her time to work out her frustrations before he patted the side of her beak and stroked her head.

After a few moments, she quieted down and allowed him to inspect her wounds. She was fortunate that the mud of the bog had softened the fall through the trees, or her injuries would have been far worse. Her chest and back were caked in dry blood. Fox inspected her wings and found them to be savagely torn, and he feared that the dragon's tail may have done more damage than he initially thought.

The falcon tried to stand, but the effort was too

great, and she fell back into the mud. With great effort Fox pulled the saddle from her back and cleared away some of the mud. His ribs ached under the strain, but he knew that this was the only way to help her. When he finally got her clear of the debris, he was relieved to see that his initial assessment was incorrect. She was hurt badly, but the wounds were not as serious as he'd feared, and they would heal if treated soon.

After resting for a few moments, they made their way slowly back to where Morwen was entrapped. The sun had set by the time they arrived at the edge of the bog, and the massive silhouette of the fallen dragon loomed just ahead of them. The young Sentinel gathered what dry wood he could find and built a small fire, primarily to keep nocturnal predators at bay. He had dragged the saddle and his riding gear with them and was glad that they had survived the crash. He rummaged through the supplies and retrieved a fairly complete medical kit so that he could tend to all of their wounds.

Fox treated Stormwise's wounds first, and as he suspected, most were superficial. Her wing was not as bad as he had feared. She wouldn't be able to fly anytime soon, but the bones appeared only to be bruised, and the wing would eventually heal as good as new. He dressed and cleaned the wounds the best he could before turning his attention to Morwen.

The great hawk had finally become conscious again when Fox began his initial examination. He helped Morwen pull himself from the mud and found that his left wing was hanging at an odd angle, and he seemed to be in pain. A quick examination revealed that one of the bones was broken, and Fox was forced to rig a makeshift sling, immobilizing the wing safely against the bird's side. The damage wasn't life-threatening, and the wing would heal, but it would be a long while before Morwen would be strong enough to fly. Fox was excited to find that the majority of the bird's wounds also appeared superficial, and he was able to clean and tend to them as he did for Stormwise.

The young elf searched through his medical kit and managed to recover enough ingredients to brew a pain reliever and healing elixir to help them all cope with their discomfort. He split what supplies he could salvage among the three of them and provided each of the birds with a light meal and some fresh water.

Morwen was in worse shape than Stormwise and was still groggy from the ordeal, but both of the birds consumed the food along with the elven healing elixir.

Fox made them as comfortable as possible and waited patiently for the natural sedative effect of the medicine to help ease them to sleep. Finally he turned his attention to himself and did what he could to cleanse and dress his own wounds--lastly wrapping his ribcage with what remained of the medical kit.

When he was done, Fox brewed a medicinal tea with the remains of the healing elixir and stoked the fire for what he thought was going to be a long night. He figured that they were about as safe as they could be in the Swamp of Doom and Despair. It would be days before the local predators would dare wander into the dragon's territory, even if they suspected him to be dead. There was nothing more he could do that evening. The last thing he remembered before giving in to pain and exhaustion was something about not falling asleep with a head wound.

****

-Chapter Eleven-

Nawg

Drago flew the green dragon to near exhaustion. Only for fear of his own safety did he finally land the beast on the plains south of the Karnel Mountains. At this rate, another day and a half on wing would bring them to the doorstep of the ogre kingdom, and that much closer to his dear old friend King Flangor.

As a race, dragons have a keen sense about the mountains, and Drago was no exception. Over the ages he had also gathered a storehouse of knowledge about the countryside, and in particular, the mountain ranges that bordered it. This knowledge base contained many secret locations in the hills and countless trails of which few others were aware. Drago knew that these little bits of information gave him a strategic advantage over enemies, and one never knew when some bit of information might come in handy.

It just happened that one of these was an oft-overlooked trail that led secretly up to the backdoor of the mountain the ogres called their home. There had been little need to visit the ogre king before; he had kept his nose out of Drago's business, and as a food source ogres weren't a particularly tasty species. With the knowledge of the Wyrd, however, everything had changed, and now Drago needed a favor from his old friend.

Somehow he doubted the king would be very happy to see him. He also very much doubted that he would be recognized in this new body, so he needed a plan to get into the mountain… but nothing came to mind until he found Eldin's cloak buried among the other effects in the elf's riding gear.

It took a little probing of his host's memories of the cloak's uses and camouflaging abilities, but in the end he learned how to use it. Once he knew what he could use it for, a devious plan came to mind. With the cloak on, he could sneak his way past any sentries that might be guarding the hidden path and slip into the mountain, using the hidden entrance. With this cloak he could be inside the belly of the beast, so to speak, before they even knew he was around.

This Sentinel was surprising him more and more every day that they shared this body. What an extraordinary find, and how fortunate that he had brought along such an interesting assortment of tools. They would come in very handy, indeed.

The stars were shining bright in the sky, and Drago breathed in the cool evening air. He flexed his muscles and stretched his back. He was sore from days in the saddle, but nearly all of his strength had returned. By the time he reached the ogres, he would be at a hundred percent. It was strange not being a dragon in form, but this little human body was proving to be stronger than he could have imagined.

Drago's magic had eventually broken through the mental walls that the former sole inhabitant of the body had built. Then he was able to begin tapping into the wealth of information that this elf had in his mind. He realized how greatly fate had truly blessed him when he discovered that this particular elf was a champion among his people and guardian of some of their greatest secrets. His knowledge of the key, alone, was enough to bring a tear to the former dragon's eye.

With the *key* he could obtain the *Wyrd,* and with that in his possession, nothing in the world would be out of his reach.

What a fantastic bonus it had been to learn that this soft little human could also fight like a dragon, as evidenced when he had defeated Drago in battle. The ancient dragon had realized early on that he would ultimately lose the fight. He was old--very, very old--and his physical body was fading, but his mind and magic were still strong. He had only to inhabit a new body, and his existence in the world could continue on indefinitely.

The magic required to accomplish this feat was very dangerous and extremely risky, so he had waited until the right opportunity arose. This elf seemed to be the perfect vehicle for his purpose, but he knew that the Sentinel would not give in willingly, so he fought to the death with the sole intention of weakening the man until his resistance was at its lowest. In the end' the dangerous scheme had worked, and Drago had cheated death by escaping his physical body and taking possession of the weakened mind of the elf when he himself had been near death.

Drago glanced up at the vast mountains looming on the horizon before him. He had conjured up a devious little plan to recover the Wyrd… but first things first. Step one was to persuade the ogres to help him. He slid the exquisite elven sword from its sheath and swung the blade outward, slicing through the trunk of a young tree and cleaving it in half in one swift stroke. The false Sentinel smiled as a large section of the tree nearly as big around as his leg fell to the ground in front of him with a thud.

Persuading the ogres shouldn't be too much trouble.

Fox awoke the next morning with a screaming headache. The sun had risen only a few minutes earlier, covering the swamp in a swathe of yellow light. He squinted his eyes against the morning brightness and tried in vain to stretch his aching muscles. His body felt as if it had been hit by a runaway dragon… and he remembered that it quite literally had. He was fortunate that his wounds weren't more serious. This fortune was most likely attributable to his fast reflexes, years of training, and physical strength. Needless to say, however, he would be in deep trouble if he didn't get out of this swamp soon.

He spied Stormwise and Morwen just beginning to stir. He decided to give them time to wake fully before they set out on their long trek, and before leaving he also wanted to find evidence of what had happened to Eldin.

Stiff from pain, he rose with great effort and groaned as he went to investigate the dead dragon's corpse. Hundreds of footprints were strewn all over the area, but he deduced that they were simply his and Eldin's, left during the fight.

Starting at the dragon's head, he followed a circular pattern, moving in an ever-increasing spiral in an attempt to determine where the prints ended. After a few minutes of searching, he had marked the outer perimeter of the battle. Only a few prints remained, and they led away from the fight into a small clearing a short distance away. Another set of tracks led away from the clearing and back in the direction of the spot where Morwen had been trapped the night before.

He knelt down to the ground and examined the tracks more closely, soon realizing that the prints leading into the clearing were considerably deeper than the others. From this he deduced that Eldin must have been carrying a great load with him at the time. Fox looked in the direction of the hawk and realized that his saddle and riding gear were missing. Had he spotted this last night? His head hurt too much to remember.

Fox followed the prints and stopped when he noticed a new set of tracks, isolated to just a few feet inside the clearing. He recognized them immediately as dragon tracks, but they were too small to have been created by the dead black. It appeared that they were fairly fresh, and Eldin's footprints circled around them. Some of his master's tracks were shallower than others, and Fox gathered from the arrangement that he must have placed Morwen's harness on this dragon, alleviating the weight he was carrying. He examined the dragon tracks a little more closely and was able to surmise that the beast had flown out of the clearing again, making a short running start before taking off. Those tracks appeared deeper than they had in the other locations. The dragon had apparently taken off with a heavy load--by all indications, with Eldin on its back--*but why?*

Fox heard a commotion and turned to see the birds rooting around the camp, apparently looking for food. Fox returned to them and broke out a small portion of the supplies. There wasn't much left, so they would have to conserve what they had in order to make it back to Greylok. In his condition there wasn't much he could do about Eldin, and his first priority was to get himself and the birds out of this swamp in one piece.

Fox knew that Eldin would have to take care of himself. If Fox could make it back to Greylok, a search party would be sent out; and when his wounds healed, he himself would go searching, if necessary. There were still a lot of questions to be answered, but for the moment they would have to wait.

With great effort Fox gathered together their supplies from the small camp and split the load equally between Morwen and Stormwise. They had recovered somewhat after their ordeal the previous day, and Fox was infinitely relieved to see that they could walk with relatively little pain. It appeared that most of their wounds were limited to their delicate wings, and though neither bird would be able to fly anytime soon, both would recover if they could just get out of the swamp.

Fox fished through his pack and recovered a short line of rope to attach to the harnesses of both birds. His body ached, and his broken ribs made even the simplest task difficult, but he realized that this was the only way to get out of this dreadful place. He explained the situation to the birds as well as he could, along with what he wanted them to do. They were intelligent creatures and understood what he was on about. His natural gift with the living things of the world enabled the young elf to touch them on a subconscious level, and they trusted in him. By the time he had the rope attached to both birds, he felt confident that they would follow wherever he led.

Fox removed a compass from his pack and referenced it against a map of the area. Eldin had taken with him a far better map, but the young Sentinel was glad he still had anything at all. He studied the figures for a few moments and was able to glean where the three of them were currently. From that he approximated the best route out of the swamp and estimated that, if all went well, they should be able to clear it by mid-afternoon. Hopefully they could make camp close to where he and Eldin had landed on their journey to the outer islands.

Fox's keen eyes spotted a rough-cut animal trail that snaked through the swamp in the general direction they needed to go. It was going to be difficult, but within a few moments the trio was on their way.

Drago hardly gave his green dragon a chance to recover before they were back on wing. He pointed the young beast in the direction of the Karnel Mountains and pushed it hard for the rest of the day, stopping only when he thought it might drop out of the air from exhaustion. When they reached the vast mountain range, he forced his mount to climb high into the sky, higher than the tallest peaks, and deep into the surrounding clouds. They landed on a shrouded summit and waited there. As night fell on the following day, he brought the dragon down into the mountains, landing it in a shallow ravine surrounded by ancient hardwood trees.

Drago commanded the dragon to keep hidden amongst the trees and to rest and regain what strength it could. It was permitted to hunt for food while he was away, but by all means it was to stay hidden from sight and do everything possible to keep its presence undetected.

Drago knew very well that dragons could stay hidden away if they wanted to. The only inhabitants of the area were ogres and trolls, and even he, with relatively poorer elf senses, could smell them coming from miles away. If the green managed to get captured, it would get what it deserved and would make a good meal for the locals--but Drago still needed the beast, so he whispered some advice into its ear and reminded it who was boss.

The false Sentinel gathered supplies from Eldin's gear and packed them into a light backpack. He found the great elven cloak hidden deep within one of the saddlebags, perfectly camouflaged with worn brown leather. He slipped the cloak around his new body and admired how it blended seamlessly into the surroundings. In conjunction with Drago's own knowledge of the terrain, Eldin's memories had provided him knowledge of how to use the cloak to become invisible. The ogre king would quite literally never see him coming.

Drago pulled on the backpack and adjusted the straps so that they wouldn't interfere with his sword. He studied the terrain for a moment and found the hidden path that he sought. The trail wound its way nearly straight up the steep mountain, hardly visible to any but the keenest eye. Its sole purpose was to allow the ogres' ruler to slip away from his mountain stronghold if his kingdom were under attack. It remained a well-guarded secret, known to only a select few in the King's personal service and those others who, like Drago, desired such useful information simply because it might one day come in handy.

Fox pushed the birds as hard as possible on foot. He did everything he could to keep them out of harm's way, but all along he had an unmistakable feeling of being spied upon by unseen eyes that followed every move they made.

The wet marsh eventually began to give way to firmer, drier ground, and they were able to make fairly good progress. By early afternoon they stopped in a small clearing to rest and eat what little food they had left.

For the most part, the inhabitants of the swamp hadn't troubled them, but Fox couldn't shake the strange feeling of being watched. The dense canopy allowed only traces of light to filter through the trees, intensifying the dark and foreboding atmosphere. He knew the birds were on edge and would have been much more at home in the sky than wandering through a swamp on foot. They were coping well with their wounds and had followed the young elf without any great trouble, but it wouldn't take much to spook them.

On the other hand, Fox himself was not doing quite as well. It was taking every bit of his strength just to keep pressing on, and he didn't know how long he could keep up the pace.

For a time his nervousness passed, but by early evening the eerie feeling returned, and his keen instincts went into overdrive. With great effort he pulled his sword from his sheath and peered into the nearby woods. Crimson eyes gazed out from the deep shadows of the surrounding forest. The ever-present mist clung to the trees, preventing him from getting a good look at the pursuers. He could discern only their menacing eyes, glowing red with malevolence and hunger. He counted at least seven, and more may have been surrounding him and his party. He readied his sword and backed the birds into the crook of a large tree so that he might get a better chance to defend them and himself.

At the edge of the forest, the glowing eyes shifted back and fourth, moving closer to the light. They were close enough now that the young Sentinel could catch fleeting glimpses of silhouettes, the massive bodies only partly hidden in the mist.

The first grotesque, boar-like creature stepped into the early evening light, snuffling at the air cautiously with its piggish snout. It was big, much bigger than Fox would have preferred. The top of its head rose nearly five feet in the air. The beast was generally wedge-shaped, with massive shoulders and an arched back that tapered downward to well-muscled hindquarters. It had muddy, coarse, yellow fur with black splotches over its haunches and spine. A black mane of bristling hair surrounded the front portion of its grizzled body and continued down the spine in a crest that ran the length of its back. The creature grunted and scratched at the earth with cloven feet, brandishing its fangs and gleaming boar's tusks.

Fox took a defensive posture and prepared himself for the onslaught. These creatures were looking for an easy meal, but he decided that they weren't going to get it. Two more of the foul beasts stepped out of the misty shadows, taking their places on either side and slightly behind the first one. They grunted and snorted, making a sickening noise that sounded almost like laughter--but hadn't the least bit of humor in it. The big one in the middle eyed Fox with furious, demonic eyes and nudged the creature on its left. The other beast twitched in anticipation and stamped at the ground, uttering more unnatural laughter. A moment later the yowling ceased, and it kicked up a cloud of dirt, charging toward Fox and the two raptors.

Fox watched as the beast ran at him, noting subconsciously that many more of the horrific creatures were stepping out of the mist to watch the scene unfold. It crashed through the brush and careened toward him with tremendous speed, brandishing its teeth and dipping its head in an attempt to ram him against a tree. An instant before the beast could collide with Fox, he sidestepped out of the way, at the same time slashing upward with his elven sword. The blade carved a thin layer of skin from the creature's soft, fleshy snout, completely unsettling it.

Fox had heeded Eldin's teachings well. Lest the circumstances were truly desperate, he should not use his talents to kill. The defensive move had the desired effect. The creature slammed into the tree at full steam, completely missing Fox and knocking itself unconscious.

Fox looked over at Stormwise and Morwen and shook his head. "At least they're not very bright."

Morwen then grabbed the limp creature in his massive clawed foot and tossed it to the side.

The remaining beasts began to approach, albeit more cautiously than the first, and soon surrounded the elf and the two birds, preventing any chance of escape. For a moment nothing happened while the two groups stared each other down, watching for the slightest sign of weakness. It only took Stormwise shifting her weight slightly to trigger the attack, and they all came at them with blinding speed.

The beasts clawed and bit at the young Sentinel, trying everything possible to get a piece of either him or the birds. Fox slashed and cut with his sword in perfect precision, slicing away at the creatures and using his skill with the blade to prevent striking them with mortal wounds.

Unfortunately Fox's injuries were getting the better of him, and he was beginning to slow down. The creatures took advantage of this and were soon gaining the upper hand, landing hit after hit. Morwen and Stormwise aided as best they could, clawing and biting the monsters with their massive beaks and talons and breaking through the ranks to slow their progress, but their strength was also beginning to ebb.

At the edge of the forest, green eyes illuminated the mist. For a moment they watched the encounter, admiring the precision and skill of the elf and his birds. Then, with barely a nod from their leader, they attacked.

The young Sentinel was quickly tiring and had made a conscious decision to strike down the boar creatures. He knew that this was now his only choice; either they fell, or he and the birds would die--kill or be killed, as it is said. Then Fox glanced up from the assault, and for an instant, caught a glimpse of massive black shapes leaping into the fray.

He positioned his blade to strike down the nearest boar creature, but the beast was suddenly torn away from the exhausted elf, and the remaining attackers began to back off. A moment later, the largest wolves he had ever seen surrounded him, and lying at their feet were the remains of his attackers.

-Chapter Twelve-

Dragons and Ogres and Wolves, Oh My!

Drago followed the mountain trail for nearly two hours as it wound its way into the misty upper reaches of unforgiving terrain. By the looks of the trail, it hadn't been used in a very long time. He scrutinized the ground for signs of anything passing, but he came across only a few animal tracks, and those looked many weeks old.

Drago closed in on the top of the mountain and the end of the trail. The path stopped at a sheer vertical wall that extended fifteen feet upward to the peak of the mountain.

When he got to the top, he drew his sword and searched quietly for the concealed opening. He was wearing Eldin's camouflaging cloak and doubted that anyone had detected his presence, but he kept his guard up just in case. For nearly a half an hour he searched the wall for any sign of an entrance. Finally he found what he was looking for in a small, seemingly insignificant crack that ran vertically along the cliff face.

He traced the crack with his fingers and was able to discern the square outline of a door etched into the wall. He had to admire the exquisite workmanship of the craftsman who had carved the entrance. If he had not known of its existence, he would probably never have come across it. From the looks of it, it was most definitely dwarven, and some poor fellow had most likely been forced to perform the task at knifepoint. Drago knew the Ogre King well enough, he grinned, and scanned the rocky terrain for some sign of the unmarked grave where the body of that dwarf must yet lie.

It took another ten minutes before the false Sentinel found the latch to release the lock on the door and some more time to disarm a deadly trip-wire that would have released a poisoned dart into his neck. Eventually the uninvited guest was satisfied that he had uncovered all the traps. He sprang the lock and slid the door open on its silent hinges.

As he lit a torch from Eldin's pack, Drago hesitated just a moment at the threshold and listened to the darkness beyond the doorframe before stepping into the side of the mountain.

Fox found himself staring into the green eyes of a fierce-looking wolf that stood nearly as tall a full-grown horse. He gulped out loud, subconsciously tightening his grip on his sword as he counted at least ten of the monstrous creatures surrounding him and the two birds.

Out of the frying pan and into the fire, he thought, but at least they had taken care of his other troubles.

The big wolf eyed the Sentinel for a moment and sat lazily back on its haunches. "Relax, elf friend. We mean you no harm."

Fox shook his head, digesting both the words and the fact that he understood completely what the giant wolf was saying.

The wolf seemed to smile in the way only an animal can and continued, "I am the King of the Dire Wolves. The creatures that attacked you are called the Nawg. They are a scourge on the land, and we've been tracking them for more than a week, but until now they managed to stay just out of our reach.

"My scouts picked up your scent and that of another elf and the raptors in the field where you did battle against the black dragon. The smell of blood from your wounds is strong, and the Nawg must also have picked up your trail. They would have attacked sooner, but they enjoy stalking and watching their prey for hours--even days before attacking. Your wounds are getting the best of you, and they must have sensed your weakness."

After hearing the wolf's words, Fox relaxed slightly and allowed his defenses to lower. It was true that his wounds ached to the point that he felt he might collapse at any moment, but he tried to hide it as best he could.

"I'm glad you came when you did. The battle with the black dragon nearly defeated me. It ambushed us as we flew overhead, driving us out of the sky and forcing us to defend ourselves."

The dire wolf nodded. "Yes that is his usual tactic. His name is Drago, and he is considered by some to be the oldest of his kind. It is said that he was born before time was marked on any calendar, and his magic is nearly unequaled... but nothing can live forever, and his physical body was weakening. He was getting too old to carry on."

Fox looked slightly hurt, and the wolf must have sensed this.

"Please do not misunderstand me. Your defeat of the dragon was most impressive. Only a few in the world could have accomplished what the two of you did, and that is exactly what concerns me.... Drago's magic is strong, and he would have sensed your skill. Even as appetizing as your birds might have looked, I doubt that he would have attacked unless he had something more on his mind than food," said the wolf.

Fox nodded, trying to understand what exactly this creature was saying to him. "You mentioned the other elf. Were you able to find him or pick up his scent?"

The dire wolf shook his head. "No, there is no elf other than you within many miles. We neither found his body nor picked up his scent. There is no other around, and this has me troubled...." The huge wolf hesitated for a moment, thinking how to continue. "Drago is not dead. His physical body lies at the edge of the marsh, decomposing in the afternoon sun, but Drago's soul has not passed on. The body is nothing more than a casing, a vehicle that carried the black soul of Drago for countless eons, but nonetheless it's just an empty shell."

Fox fell to his knees, both from physical exhaustion and from the dark thoughts running through his head. "What exactly are you saying? What could have happened to Eldin?"

Looking deeply worried, the dire wolf paused, giving the boy an extra moment to contemplate the implications. "I have no proof of what I imagine, but I doubt that it is a coincidence that both your compatriot and Drago are absent. It is within his power to take possession of another being of a different form. The battle was probably nothing more than a way to weaken your companion's mind and bring him close to death. In this state, your friend's mental defenses would be down, allowing Drago to slip in and take control."

Fox felt defeated. The events of the last two days had caught up with him, and he was only moments from collapse. "I believe what you say. Eldin would never have left my side. Something must have happened, but I am simply too weak to help him. I need to get these birds back to Greylok and to heal my wounds before I can search for my master."

The dire wolf nodded. His senses and his very nature made him keenly aware of the young elf's extensive wounds. In his estimation, it attested only to the boy's noble character that he was able to fight the Nawg and defend the birds with wounds from a battle that had defeated a black dragon... even if only in the flesh. This elf truly deserved the title of friend.

"Please allow us to help," said the King of the Dire Wolves.

Fox looked up at the King and smiled. A moment later, too exhausted to remain conscious, he passed out.

Dark thoughts raced through Drago's mind as he crept through the uninhabited passage of the ogres' mountain. For more than an hour, he wandered down the seemingly forgotten hall with no sign of pursuit.

Old King Flangor has truly gotten smug in his mountain stronghold. It's about time to stir the pot.

Drago was lost in his own thoughts when a foul

scent came to him. He hesitated for a moment, sniffing the air and listening to the darkness. It didn't take an especially keen nose to smell the locals, and he knew he was getting close.

His plan was simple. Using the magnificent cloak, he would slip into King Flangor's throne room, eliminating anyone who stood in his way, and present to his dear old friend a business opportunity that he couldn't possibly refuse.

Drago extinguished his torch and allowed his elven eyes to adjust to the dim light as he listened to at least two ogres arguing with each other a short distance away. The voices carried up the narrow passage, and from the sound of it he seriously doubted they had any indication of his presence.

Their voices seemed muffled, and Drago assumed that the passage was most likely concealed from them. He crept down the dark tunnel, listening to the argument as they became more agitated with one another. At this rate he could probably have walked right past them without any notice, even without the invisibility cloak, but he opted to have a little fun instead.

Drago reached the end of the tunnel and stopped at a rock wall. He searched the edges with his fingers and once again detected a rectangular crack that traced the outline of a door. After a moment's search, he was able to locate the release mechanism and carefully opened the door. It slid open on silent hinges onto a recessed alcove slightly off the main tunnel. Light flooded into the passageway, exposing the opening, but because of its location it was out of eyeshot of the arguing ogres. Drago smiled at his luck and slipped out of the tunnel, closing the secret door behind him.

The ogres weighed at least three hundred pounds each and had filthy gray-green flesh, shaggy black hair, and beady little eyes set deep in their bulbous heads. Each had overgrown pointy ears, a broad nose, and two blunt but almost tusk-like teeth protruding upward from their lower jaws. They were currently spraying spittle in every direction while screeching at each other.

Using the cloak for cover, Drago slid up behind the closer of the two creatures, his movements perfectly concealed by the camouflaging capability of the garment. Without a second thought, he lifted Eldin's sword with both hands and slammed the blunt butt end of the weapon into the back of the creature's head.

The ogre didn't know what hit him; he fell forward, unconscious, into the arms of the brute he'd been arguing with.

"Get off me, Slag! You think I'll let you win if you fake falling asleep? Wake up, and we'll settle this argument once and for all!"

Drago smiled and shoved the unconscious creature forward, knocking both of them to the ground. He leapt over the fallen goons and took off down the hall, laughing hysterically and leaving one unconscious and one very confused ogre in his wake.

Fox awoke in his bed back at Greylok, aching all over. He checked his wounds gingerly. Most of his body was swathed in clean white cloth that had the distinctive aroma of medicinal herbs, and his ribs and his head were both wrapped tightly in a similar material. He had no more than a few hazy memories of what had happened, but he vaguely remembered being carried on the back of a giant wolf and lying in a field of wildflowers just before being rescued by an elf scouting party.

Pretty much everything else since the battle with the dragon was just a blur. He dimly remembered fighting the Nawg and that the dire wolves had helped him, but even that wasn't too clear.

Fox rubbed his head and slid his legs over the side of the bed. He tried to stand, but as soon as his feet touched the floor, he became dizzy and fell backwards onto the bed, knocking out of his lungs what little wind had been in them. He closed his eyes with a groan, and mercifully, slipped back into dreamland.

Eldin's cloak allowed Drago to slip easily through the complex networks of caverns without detection. He knew that King Flangor's hall was situated near the center of the vast mountain complex. As a former dragon, he had a natural instinct for navigating caves, so he had little fear of not locating the throne room quickly.

For the most part, the ogre kingdom was awash with filth and foul smells. Torches mounted on the cavern walls poured smoke into the air, staining the walls black with grime and making visibility and breathing difficult. The air reeked of decomposing garbage, as the inhabitants tossed their refuse into the tunnels, attracting rats and breeding disease in the countless piles of decomposing filth.

Between the foul stench and the lack of visibility, even the false Sentinel's finely tuned instincts were struggling to assist him with navigation. Eventually his exploration uncovered a long, well-lit tunnel that differed distinctly from the other passages he'd passed through. He hesitated at the entrance to this new tunnel, lurking unseen in the deep shadows and watching the ogres that were stationed there. He noted immediately that not only was the tunnel clean and smoke-free, but even the ogres there looked different. They were well-armed with long swords and battle pikes. They stood two by two in an orderly fashion, wearing ornate leather battle gear adorned with medals and symbols of rank.

In all he counted ten of the well-armed thugs, and he knew immediately that he had found what he was looking for. Drago pushed deeper into the shadows and flexed his muscles while removing Eldin's cloak. He didn't need the extra advantage that the cloak provided to eliminate this hurdle, and he wanted to see what he could do on his own.

The false Sentinel stepped into the light, withdrawing his sword from its sheath. "Hello, gentlemen. I'd like to have a chat with your king."

The ogres looked up in unison. Drago presumed that it was their leader who spoke first.

"Where'd you come from?"

Drago smiled and moved a little deeper into the hall. He needed to get to the end of the passage at which stood a large, ornate wooden door that would gain him entrance to the throne room.

The Captain of the guard withdrew his own sword and quickly regained his composure. "I don't think our King wants to see you, unless you have an appointment...." The ogre examined the false Sentinel, analyzing him from head to toe. Finally he grinned at the elf with a set of rotten yellow teeth, "...and I doubt he would bother to grant an elf an appointment anyhow."

Drago grinned back and twirled his sword in his hand. "Well I guess we'll just have to do this the hard way."

The leader of the ogres smashed his pike into

the floor. "Rid me of this scum, but save the sword… it looks valuable."

The first two ogres in line charged Drago, thrusting their pikes at both his feet and his head, but the false Sentinel easily dodged the attack, rotating slightly on his heels and slashing upward with his sword at the same time. In a perfectly fluid motion, the blade of his sword sliced through the pikes, dropping them harmlessly to the floor while Drago shifted his body away from the ogres.

He smiled for a half second, repositioning himself perfectly in a position behind the two attackers, who had been caught completely off guard by the maneuver. They turned to resume the attack, but Drago had already begun the offensive and in an instant eliminated the foes in two quick jabs. Unlike Eldin, trapped deep inside this elf body, Drago felt no remorse for his actions; he cared little for the lives of others and used or defeated them as he saw fit.

Stunned for only a moment, the next four ogres in line then charged at the false Sentinel. They raced down the hall, dropping their pikes and unsheathing their swords. They stopped just in front of Drago, giving him a wide birth.

Drago hesitated for only a second, lowering his sword and relaxing his arm so that the tip of the blade was only inches from the floor. The ogres used this moment to attack, and they raised their curved blades and swung at the elf.

Effortlessly, Drago blended with the attack, spinning away from the blow while rotating the blade and slicing upward into the attackers exposed arms, immediately eliminating two of the four foes. An instant later he twisted at the waist, and with the back-cut of the same stroke, followed through, with the sword slicing across the backs of the remaining two attackers.

Without the need to look back, Drago stepped away from a growing pile of incapacitated guards and strolled casually farther down the hall. Three of the remaining four ogres lowered their pikes, pointing them directly at Drago's chest and effectively blocking any further progress he could make. The false Sentinel took one step back and kneeled slowly, laying his sword on the ground. In the next moment, he leapt to his feet and grabbed the business end of the middle pike with both hands and thrust it back into the ogre who was holding it. He rotated his hips, twisting the pike and at the same time wrenching it away from the helpless attacker.

Now standing between the two other aggressors, he thrust his newly acquired pike into the ogre on the left and then, without hesitating, pulled it free and drove it into the man on the right. An instant later he dropped to his knees and rolled away from the stunned guards as he reached for his sword and hopped back to his feet.

Drago surged forward, moving the elven blade in a circular arc, and in one motion finished off his adversaries. He then stood face to face with the captain of the guard. Without a moment's hesitation, Drago whirled the blade in the air and removed this final obstacle before the ogre had a chance even to blink.

Drago kicked open the heavy wooden door and stepped into King Flangor's throne room. The room was brightly lit and was adorned with rich carpets and luminous tapestries that covered the floor and hung from the roughly hewn rock walls. Trays of food and wine were piled on finely crafted tables in the middle of the room, within easy reach of the King and his advisors. The King and a few of his minions were busily stuffing their faces, apparently oblivious to any commotion outside the room.

King Flangor had apparently been trying unsuccessfully to cram the leg of some unidentifiable creature into his mouth when the door flew open. "What is the meaning of this intrusion?" he demanded, as a steady stream of half-chewed food poured from his lips.

Drago stepped into the room, smiling. He held in his fist a long, filthy ponytail that was still attached to the lifeless head of the Captain of the King's Guard. Drago swung the head around in the air and tossed it onto the table of food. It rolled across the polished wood and came to rest just in front of the King, seeming to stare at the fat monarch with sightless eyes.

Drago scanned the room with disgust. "Gentlemen--and I use the term loosely--I'd like you to help me rob a bank." He allowed the ogres to take a good look at the severed head. "As you can see, I don't take no for an answer."

-Chapter Thirteen-

Just Business

Nearly a fortnight had passed since Fox had returned from the Swamp of Doom and Despair. His body was repairing itself nicely, but the elf healers would not allow him to return to duty to look for Eldin. He had done everything he could do from Greylok, long distance, but none of the search parties or scouting missions he'd sent out had provided any news of Eldin's whereabouts.

Fox had heeded the dire wolf's warning well. He was concerned that his mentor might have been possessed by the black dragon's dark spirit, but without proof there was little he could do. He had gone to Enob, the King's High Wizard, but even he could do nothing to disprove the wolf's theory. They could only play a waiting game until the missing Sentinel surfaced.

A few days before Fox had returned from the swamp, the King had managed to get himself in some serious trouble. He had believed he was drinking a medicinal tea, which he thought would help him cure a headache, but had inadvertently consumed a potion that would slowly turn him into stone. Since it was an emergency situation, and Eldin and Fox were away, Enob had sought help from the city of Cloudview and its Incantation Enforcement Agency's Counter-Curse Division.

After analyzing the King's condition, Enob and the two agents from the Counter-Curse Division had determined that they would need to create an antidote to counteract the toxin running through he King's veins. Neither Enob nor the spell-breaking detectives had all the ingredients for the antidote on hand, and they had been forced to trek across the country in search of a talon from one of only two blood dragons in existence.

Normally this task would have been assigned to the Sentinels, but because both Eldin and Fox had been in action at the time, the job of accompanying the detectives had fallen to an elf ranger. Coincidentally this just happened to be Fox's uncle, Asher Strongbow. Although Fox could think of no one better able to handle the task, it still made him feel awful that he hadn't been able to do his own job to help the King escape a perilous condition.

Between being helpless in the search for Eldin and unable to aid the King, the young Sentinel was feeling very bad indeed. After a couple of weeks had passed, he found himself sulking the days away while doing everything he could think of to keep himself busy. He checked on both Morwen and Stormwise daily. They were doing much better since their ordeal in the swamp. Most of their injuries had healed, but it would still be a week or more before Morwen would be able to fly.

Stormwise, on the other hand, had faired better than Fox could have imagined and had healed well enough to take flight. He yearned to join her in her aerial exploits, but his healing process prevented him from doing so. Instead, he found himself occupying his time on the practice field, trying to improve his archery skills.

In archery practice, the arrow and the target became the young Sentinel's only focus. For a moment the world around him ceased to exist. From his perspective, time moved in slow motion when he released the bowstring, watching as the arrow eased smoothly away from the bow and sailed skyward effortlessly. The lazy arc of its flight seemed to drag on for an eternity, but finally, with a *crack,* the world raced back into real time, and he could see the sharply flaked arrowhead tear into its mark before he reached back and withdrew another from his quiver.

As he practiced one particular afternoon, a soft breeze blew across the knee-high grass, which undulated like green waves over the gently sloping archery range. In the distance a flock of small birds erupted from the trees, and a dark shadow passed overhead just as the elf tore another hole in the distant target. A blood-red dragon flew gracefully above the field, and Fox's keen eyes spotted his uncle riding on its back, accompanied by what looked like a human boy and a dog.

He hadn't been taking any pain medication for nearly a week, and no one had sent any spells his way, so he was fairly sure he wasn't hallucinating. In a rush the events of the past couple of weeks exploded in his mind, and he grabbed his quiver and took off after the dragon. It was heading straight for the castle, and even if he were in shape to run flat-out, it would arrive long before he could.

The ancient lock snapped open with a *click,* and the shrouded figure groaned as the dim light from his lantern illuminated the tunnel ahead. A day before, he'd slipped into the Great Forest, Eldin's camouflaging cloak shifting with the surrounding foliage as if it were continually being painted to match the environment. He had to give the elves credit. They were good at patrolling their lands and keeping watch for those who did not belong there, and even with the aid of the cloak, he was forced to make a wide berth around them.

Through some probing of Eldin's memories, Drago knew exactly where he was going, and he found the small grove of slender aspen trees easily enough, nestled within the massive trunks surrounding it. Even Drago couldn't resist their beauty, marveling at their appearance and how strikingly they resembled bleached bones. He envisioned himself within a forest of living skeletons surrounded by giants, but he knew that in the midst of the proud aspens he would find the secret entrance to the elf city far above the ground.

The nearly invisible entrance was actually located in an oak tree that had rotted to the core and nearly fallen in upon itself. In its prime, the tree must have been splendid--full and tall, with a broad trunk and wide-reaching canopy. Now rotted and hollow, it simply stood in stark contrast with the aspens.

The hatch was not large, by any stretch, but the false Sentinel slipped through it easily and climbed down the narrow, root-encrusted shaft. The passage opened wide and branched off in a number of directions, following the roots of the trees, but the main trail was clear and easy to follow. The air was cool and damp, and he followed the tunnel using Eldin's memories until the flickering lamplight illuminated the ancient rungs of a ladder that rose far overhead.

Drago strapped a leather cord to his lantern and draped it over his shoulder. He grabbed hold of one of the rungs and began the long climb up the ladder. It rose for what seemed an eternity, extending thousands of feet within the enormous tree. In his new body, Drago was in perfect physical condition, but even so the climb nearly exhausted him. If it weren't for periodic platforms where he could rest, the effort might simply have been too much. As it was, he skipped as many of these stops as he could to quicken his ascent, but it still took many hours to reach the top.

On the way up, he had some time to reflect on the past couple of weeks. First he'd had the fortune to transfer his living soul into this body. It was an unimaginable bonus that this insignificant little elf had knowledge of the Wyrd and the location of the key to release it from the vault in which it resided!

Only a handful of beings knew of the Wyrd's existence, and only a few knew were it had been hidden; but even Drago had not known what had happened to the key. Without it he was helpless to break through the lock that bound the Wyrd. But against all odds, this elf knew of the key and how to retrieve it, and with that knowledge a plan quickly formed in the false Sentinel's devious mind.

The history of the Wyrd was a long-forgotten tale. According to legend it had been etched on a stone tablet and buried eons ago in a vast cavern system, to be hidden away for all eternity. Countless generations later, the city of Cloudview was built directly above the cavern. …As Drago knew, it was a universally accepted axiom that something must always be built over a secret location. During construction of the city, the cave had been barricaded, and the builders had presumably constructed some structure over the ancient entrance.

The first step in his plan had come together nicely, and with the help of King Flangor he was able to rob the Gold Trust Bank, procuring a map to the location of this long-forgotten entrance and what was currently on top of it.

With this accomplished, only two more tasks remained. The first was to recover the key from the impenetrable elven vault in the city of Greylok, and the second was to locate the Wyrd itself.

His ascent finally ended at a heavy iron trapdoor that appeared not to have been tampered with for centuries. He pressed the door open, and a wary glance through the crack revealed a large, deserted storage closet, apparently long forgotten. Wiggling and wedging himself up through the doorway, he was able to squeeze into the room. He stood still and listened intently for anyone who might have heard him, then began to examine his surroundings.

The room stood bare except for the plenitude of

cobwebs that graced its walls and ceilings. A small wooden door was the room's only entrance. Drago moved cautiously to the door and listened. Assuming Eldin's memories were correct, the door opened on a short passage that would lead him to a room that stood directly above the vault. He could hear nothing from the other side of the door, so he tested the lock. It opened smoothly with only the slightest squeals from its rusty hinges, and a quick glance down the hall confirmed that he was alone.

He slipped through the dust-filled corridor and headed in the direction of the vault. He heard a scraping sound in the distance and ducked quickly through the nearest doorway. He dropped to his knees and sneaked a look to see if he could find the source of the noise. No one could be seen, but the sound became louder as if slowly approaching him. Very cautiously he moved in the direction of the noise, relying on Eldin's cloak to keep concealed. A moment later a small cat rounded the corner just ahead of him, and Drago breathed a sigh of relief. The last thing he wanted was to alert the elves of his presence; he wanted as little interference as possible in his subsequent search for the Wyrd. If the elves realized that the key was missing, they would surely know that someone was seeking to recover it.

So far his plan had been completely successful. The robbery of the Gold Trust Bank had been executed perfectly. The fools in the city assumed that the ogres and trolls were simply attempting to rob the vaults. Drago's intent was to make it look as professional as possible by providing King Flangor and his men with weapons and detailed maps of the bank. Neither Flangor or the city officials had any inkling that his true intention was that the robbery cover his clandestine entrance into the bank's vault. It had been relatively easy selling Flangor on the idea, once he'd learned just how much gold was actually stored in there. The weapons and the maps had only sweetened the deal.

In the end, it had actually been a close call. He had expected the ogres to get inside and clean out the place, but somehow the fools had gotten themselves caught in the process. He'd barely had time to get the map out, but the cloak had once again saved him from detection.

Drago reached an old wooden door that looked as if it had not been opened in years. He turned the door handle but found it to be locked. The false Sentinel removed the proper tools from his pack and commenced work on the lock. A few moments later, it sprang open, and he quickly entered the room.

The room was actually a small armory that seemed to have been long forgotten. Swords, axes, clubs, every other weapon one might expect was stored there. According to Eldin's memory, the vault was directly below this room, so all Drago need do was find a ventilation duct in the floor. He eased himself around the maze of weaponry, searching the floor until he came across a locked metal grate, partially hidden under a weapons rack.

It took only a moment to pick the rusted lock that held the frame in place before Drago could slip into the narrow passage. To his pleasant surprise, it was large enough for him to move through comfortably, and the cool air that brushed his face was not unpleasant. He crawled through the ducting until he spotted a thin beam of light that swirled with the dust he stirred up in passing.

The next thing he saw was something he could not soon forget. Even his own vast fortune, cached underneath the Swamp of Doom and Despair, could not begin to compare with what was stored in the elven vault.

The room was enormous--he could hardly guess at its dimensions. Every possible square inch of space was heaped with wealth. Jewels and priceless antiquities lay piled in waves of color, like shimmering islands in a sea of gold. Weapons forged by masters, created from the rarest of materials, lay in countless numbers, as far as the eye could see. The very sight of the room mesmerized him. Never before in his life had he been baffled by the wealth of another, but this was beyond even his comprehension.

Drago reached out with his senses to discern any presence that might deny him this fortune, but he could not detect a soul. Gently he pushed the iron frame aside and withdrew a length of rope from his pack. He tied the end to a nearby anchor in the wall and tested it for strength. When it proved to hold his weight, he cautiously lowered himself into the sea of gold, hardly able to contain his joy.

When he touched down, he was forced to tread on the gold until he could reach a narrow path that meandered through the vast room. He followed the path until it ended in the room's only entrance, a massive, completely seamless iron door that was etched with ancient runes. As he approached the door, the runes began to glow. He drew closer, and the air seemed to thicken around him. Before he could get within five feet, the air itself became as solid as a wall of stone between him and the door.

He immediately recognized the magic as old, maybe even as old as he was. He could break it, but it would take a long time, a very long time indeed. He returned to the job at hand and searched for what he had come there to retrieve. He followed the path as it wound its way through the room until he reached a small platform on which stood a glass box on a pedestal. Within the enclosure was the item he sought.

There were items in the room considered beyond price, but even they seemed to have been cast aside, tossed into a random heap of treasure. Only this case seemed to reflect any care or concern. One quick glance around the room verified what he already knew: Amongst the unimaginable wealth, this small glass case contained the most valuable item within these walls.

Drago released a small sliver of magic and touched the case with his senses. Small runes around the base of the pedestal flared in the presence of his magic, and Drago quickly severed his connection. The false Sentinel approached the dome slowly, fearing the worst, but nothing happened. He reached out cautiously to touch the glass, and it simply felt cool to his hand. Any magic it might have contained was at bay for the time being.

He pressed the glass and lifted it away from the pedestal. There was a slight *hiss* as the air pressure in the chamber equalized, but nothing happened of note. He reached for the key and lifted it away from its resting place… and that was when everything went berserk.

Sirens blared in the distance, and the lights in the room flashed on and off blindingly.

So much for keeping this a secret!

Drago pocketed the key and took off running. He grabbed hold of the rope and climbed it as quickly as he could. He reached the ceiling and pulled the rope up behind him, sliding the metal grate back in place just as elves stormed into the vault. The false Sentinel raced through the ductwork and exited back into the empty armory, quickly closing off the duct and pulling the storage rack back in place.

So far they hadn't reached him. By now the guards had realized that the key was missing, and he knew they would leave no stone unturned until they found it. He had only a few minutes before they realized how he had gained access to the room, but he hoped that would be more than enough time. He raced out of the armory and back down the ancient, dust-filled hall, realizing that his passing had left a distinct trail of footprints on the floor, but there was little he could do about it now.

As quickly as he could, he slipped into the storage room and barred the door shut. With all his might, he heaved open the trap door and slid down the ancient ladder.

-Chapter Fourteen-

Getaway

Drago was now so close to accomplishing his goal that he couldn't afford to make a mistake. It was one thing to fight off a small brigade of fat, lazy ogres, but squad upon squad of well-trained elf rangers on their own turf was another matter indeed. He raced down the ancient tunnel, fleeing, with the elf guards in hot pursuit.

Sweat poured down his face as he pushed his new elven body to the extreme. He was running so fast that he nearly passed right under the exit to the tunnel, but at the last moment he stopped and scrambled up the tree roots.

The sun exploded into view as he slipped out of the rotted oak tree, and the light blinded him momentarily. He peered off into the distance and spotted a small company of elves who were searching for the long-forgotten tunnel entrance. They were still a good distance away, beyond the tree line of the aspen grove and halfway across a field of knee-high grass.

They had dismounted from their squirrels and were searching through the field but were clearly headed in the direction of the aspens. It would be only a few moments before either they found the entrance or the elves that had followed him from castle picked up his trail in the tunnel. Eldin's cloak would help, but these were the finest hunters and trackers in the land. They had lived their whole lives in this country and knew it as well as their own backyards. They could read the movement of an animal in dense brush as easily as if it had raced across a sandy beach and left clear, perfect tracks. The elves were no fools; they knew exactly what Drago carried, and they would employ every skill they could muster in pursuit of their quarry.

Slowly Drago retrieved the longbow from across his back and reached into his quiver for a black arrow. Delving into the memories of the one whose body he now inhabited, he traced his fingers lovingly along the edge of the arrow's raven-feathered fletching, admiring how its black sheen took on an eerie purple cast in the afternoon sun. Quietly he knocked the arrow and drew back the bowstring. He whispered an ancient, magical language into the arrow, and a series of red runes flared along its shaft a moment before he released the cord.

Sunlight glistened from the arrow's razor edges as it sailed in a deadly arc, tearing into the ground inches in front of the elf trackers. An instant later the magic flared up, and the shaft exploded into fiery fragments. The elf trackers leapt back from the explosion and watched helplessly as the fragments squirmed in the soil, quickly growing and taking the shape of flaming red serpents.

Drago watched for only a moment as seven of the magical creatures formed from the arrow. He smiled briefly and ran into the deep woods, using the distraction to gain some distance on his pursuers. There was no use in trying to conceal his tracks. The elves were simply too good at following his trail, so instead he chose to gain as much of a lead as he could.

He raced through the forest, leaping over fallen logs and crashing through ancient ferns in a mad dash for freedom. As he ran he pulled from around his neck a bone whistle on a leather strip and blew into it. No audible sound emitted from the small, white instrument, but he felt a slight shift in the magical spectrum, and he knew that his silent call had been made.

In the distance he could hear the elves still in hot pursuit and knew he was running out of time. In this body he could fight off many of them, but from the sound of it, the elves had an entire army on his trail.

He broke out of the woods and into a small clearing just as his pursuers caught up with him. He started to make his way back into the woods but found that he was completely surrounded by the relentless trackers. Many of them were riding giant squirrels, and he now realized how they had so easily followed him and evaded his deadly distraction.

The elves quickly began to tighten the circle, surrounding him with throngs of expert fighters. The false Sentinel turned and looked in every direction, but there was no sign of escape. They had surrounded him completely, so he stopped in the middle of the clearing and drew his sword.

The elves quickly closed the gap, but at the last moment the green dragon swooped into view and landed only inches away from him. Drago bounded into the saddle, and the beast leapt into the air, spraying the nearest of his attackers with a mist of acidic venom.

Fox raced to the castle as quickly as he could. He was close enough that he could see that the rare blood dragon had landed on the front lawn of the castle grounds. The young Sentinel stopped in his tracks for a second and shook his head from side to side. For the second time today he had to question his own sanity. At this distance it was hard to say for sure, but he could swear that the blood-red beast was having its claws tended to by the Queen's handmaidens.

Before he could put another thought to it, a trio of elf guards approached the young Sentinel. Seeing Fox's look of fascination, they turned their heads and followed his gaze to the dragon on the lawn. They hesitated for a moment to watch the dragon being manicured before remembering the importance of their message.

"Sir, we have just learned that the Royal Vault has been robbed, and the thief is currently being pursued through the forest below." The guard shuffled his feet for a moment and looked away from Fox before continuing. "There is no confirmation, but a number of witnesses believe it is your master, Eldin, whom they are pursuing...."

Fox turned and faced the elves. "What's been stolen?"

The tallest of the three elves spoke. "We were told only that one item of great importance is missing, but we were not made privy to what it was." The guard shrugged his shoulders and continued. "We were simply told to find you and relay this bit of information. The Master at Arms said this would be enough for you to understand."

Fox's eyes widened, and he nodded to the guard. "Yes, I understand his meaning. Where was the thief last seen?"

The guards looked directly at Fox now, surprised that he wasn't upset by the accusation against his mentor. "The latest report indicates he was pursued down an ancient service tunnel within one of the support trees, so by now he can't be far from the ground. Our best information leads us to believe that he should exit somewhere in the vicinity of Echo Lake."

Fox nodded. "I know of the tunnel. I'll go after him myself."

The young Sentinel took off at a run in the direction of Stormwise's roost but then stopped and turned again. "What news do you have of the King?" he called out.

The guards smiled in unison. "Your uncle and the agents from Cloudview returned successful," said one, "with the proper ingredient to finish the elixir. It seems that the King will recover nicely."

Fox smiled back. "Please tell my uncle that I've been called away but will plan to see him very soon!"

He then waved to the guards and dashed off. He knew that the Master at Arms was referring to *the key,* and that only Eldin would have been able to steal it. It seemed that the dire wolf's prediction was true after all.

The young Sentinel raced up the stairs into the stables and found Stormwise resting quietly in the sun. Fox was in luck--she was still wearing a weight harness that the healers had modified to help with her rehabilitation.

She perked up as soon as she saw him coming

and allowed him to approach without hesitation. Fox slid up to her and whispered into her ear. She kicked and clawed at the ground, and Fox knew she was ready for some real action. As quickly as he could, the young elf removed the extra weight from the training harness and leapt up onto her back. He didn't have the time to saddle her with a proper flight harness, so this would have to suffice.

Fox pulled hard on the reins and turned her toward the forest. With only the slightest tap of his heels, she ran down the stable's platform and leapt into the air. The wooden platform dropped away beneath them, and she soared into the canopy of giant trees.

Fox pointed her toward Echo Lake before forcing her into a dive. The air whipped through his hair as they dove toward the ground, weaving and twisting through the tree branches. When they had cleared the thick canopy and the way ahead was less congested, Stormwise pulled in her wings and accelerated her descent between the massive trunks.

Greylok was so high in the trees that, even at the tremendous velocity of a diving falcon, it took Stormwise nearly five minutes before they reached the ground. When she finally came within clear sight of the deck, she swooped out of the dive and leveled off. Fox quickly reoriented himself and spotted the elf search parties. It took him only a few seconds to get his bearings, and he pointed the falcon in the direction the elves seemed to be traveling.

Less than a minute later, she broke through a gap in the forest and into a small clearing on the edge of Echo Lake. He was a few seconds too late. The green dragon had already lifted off and was accelerating into the sky. Fox looked closely at the fleeing creature and recognized Eldin on its back.

Fox knew that retrieval of the key was of utmost importance. Regardless of who had stolen it, it had to be recovered at any cost. He made the decision to give chase, and Stormwise raced to catch up with the green dragon.

Drago turned and spotted the pursuing falcon. He recognized the bird and the young elf who rode it from the ambush in the swamp, when he had been in his former dragon body. He gleaned from his host's memories that the boy had been apprenticed to Eldin.

This boy was also a Sentinel and could be Drago's only equal in fighting skill, but with the key in his possession, today wasn't a good day to test who might come out the victor. Drago had bigger fish to fry.

He pushed the green dragon to climb faster and to lead the falcon into the massive forest in hope of losing the young elf among the trees. The dragon obeyed, tucking in its wings and slipping between tree trunks to weave its serpentine body through the towering hardwoods.

Fox and Stormwise followed. The nimble falcon was far more agile than the dragon and much more familiar with flying among the trees. She soared headlong into the forest and quickly gained on the fleeing green reptile, easily closing the gap between them.

The young Sentinel braced his legs to keep his balance and let go the falcon's reins. His bow had been slung across his back, and he grabbed it and carefully removed an arrow from his quiver. Fox quickly took aim and released the projectile, aiming directly at the green dragon's leathery wings.

Drago sensed the danger instantly and pulled

the beast hard to the left, nearly forcing it to collide with one of the massive trunks. The evasive maneuver had the proper effect, and the arrow narrowly missed its mark. Drago kicked the dragon's sides, pushing it to climb as fast as it could while banking around the tree in an attempt to make itself a more difficult target.

Aware that he had lost the element of surprise, Fox cursed to himself and withdrew another arrow. He tried to take aim, but he could see that Eldin knew exactly how to prevent his getting off an easy shot. The fleeing dragon dodged behind a group of smaller trees and was able to regain some distance between itself and the falcon. Stormwise immediately followed, pointing her head skyward in an aggressive climb and forcing Fox to give up on the bow as he was pressed back in his seat.

Stormwise was easily the faster and more maneuverable of the two flying creatures, but the dragon's huge, powerful wings gave it a slight climbing advantage over the smaller falcon. Drago used this edge to gain as much distance between them as he could--getting himself and the key out of the area took priority over eliminating the young apprentice, who could be dealt with later.

The dragon soared into the sky, weaving between the massive tree trunks and attempting every evasive maneuver in the book to stay ahead of the falcon. Still, Stormwise wouldn't give up and steadily approached the dragon, moving to within a few inches of its trailing tail. She reached out her beak and snapped at the long tail, nipping off the tip of the triangular point, including the tiniest bit of flesh under the scaly armor.

The dragon roared in pain and accelerated upward. In rage it tilted its long, reptilian head backwards and released a cone of venomous acid from between its jaws. The toxic fluid flowed upward in a tight stream, which eventually lost velocity and broke apart at the top of its arc. The dragon banked hard to the right, twisting its body aggressively to veer away from the falling cascade of its own deadly acid rain.

Fox and Stormwise spotted the toxic shower falling toward them and dove away from the deadly liquid. Stormwise pitched and flipped over as quickly as she could, contorting her body and doing her best to avoid contact with the expanding cone of fluid. The tactic helped them to avoid the bulk of the falling toxin, but they couldn't avoid it entirely and were forced to come in contact with the mist.

Fox tucked his head into his chest, and a few of the toxic drops splattered on his back, instantly burning through his clothes and into his skin. The same happened to Stormwise as she caught a few of the drops on her wings and back. They both howled in agony, momentarily giving up chase and dropping from the sky.

Drago smiled from his seat on the dragon but pushed the beast to keep climbing; he knew the young elf wouldn't give up so easily. In a moment they would be within the tangle of the branches and soon after that break free of the forest itself. He looked back and saw that the elf and falcon had already resumed the chase. All he needed was one more trick to free himself from their pursuit. He grinned and pulled the bone whistle from around his neck, blowing into the instrument as he wove some of his magic into the silent notes.

Contact with the acid had thrown Stormwise into a tumbling fall. Fox's back continued to burn from the acrid drops, but he ignored the pain and pulled hard on the flight reins, forcing Stormwise's head upward in an attempt to stop their fall. She too howled in agony but responded to the command, and they recovered from the rapid descent. Fox wrenched free his burnt outer cloak and threw it off his back. Then without concern for his own hands, he wiped away the droplets that sizzled on Stormwise's back and wings. Most of the damage had already been done, and they would be left with some scarring, but nothing was life-threatening. A moment later they swooped out of the dive, using their increased velocity to rotate skyward again and into a spiraling climb.

The dragon had already flown into the thicket within the canopy of the colossal forest. It zigzagged its way through the tangle of branches, keeping a degree of separation between itself and its pursuer. Still, the long, leathery wings of the dragon were not meant for flying within the dense canopy, and it started to loose ground once again to the nimbler falcon.

Fox and Stormwise regained most of the distance between themselves and the dragon. The falcon's shorter wingspan allowed her to slip between the tree branches and weave seamlessly upward without slowing down. Before long they had closed the gap again, forcing Eldin and the dragon into a new series of evasive maneuvers. This time the dragon was at a distinct disadvantage within the narrow confines of the maze of branches. It weaved left, then right, up and over the gigantic branches, slowly gaining altitude but continuously ripping and tearing at the delicate webbing of its leathery wings.

Understanding the importance of the situation, Stormwise pushed herself to the limit in an attempt to gain on the escaping dragon. She swerved back and forth through the tangle of branches, tucking through tight turns around the trees while knitting her way across the complex network of branches and foliage of the forest canopy. Fox lay low across her back, both to diminish the wind drag and to avoid being ripped out of his seat in any unexpected collision with the foliage.

Their extra effort paid off, and she closed the gap once again. The two aerial creatures wove through the trees, rising and diving, playing a dangerous game of cat and mouse constantly vying for the slightest advantage.

Fox grabbed the reins and pulled them back slightly, forcing the falcon upward in a course slightly above the green dragon's. He pressed his heels into her in sides, trying to squeeze out an extra ounce of effort so that they could get above the beast.

Glimpses of sunlight were projected through the thick foliage, and Fox knew they must be getting close to the tops of the trees. He had only one more chance to down the dragon before it escaped into the clear air.

Drago sensed the boy's presence overhead and kicked his heels into the dragon's sides, pushing it to climb out of the canopy. Fox released the flight reins and applied light pressure on the back of Stormwise's neck. She immediately responded to the command and tucked in her wings to become streamlined, like a missile. Fox grabbed hold of the harness as tightly as he could and let the bird do the rest.

The bird angled her head downward and realigned her trajectory directly toward the fleeing green dragon. In a nearly uncontrollable dive, she accelerated straight for the creature's back. An instant before collision, she un-tucked her wings, throwing her head back and reaching down to strike with her strong, razor-sharp talons.

Drago barely responded in time, pressing down on the back of the green dragon while forcing all his will into the evasive tactic. The dragon ducked out of the way, rolling and diving under one of the many branches before turning skyward once again. But Stormwise had anticipated the maneuver and was able to respond without hesitation. As the dragon rolled out from below the massive branch, the falcon reached out with her claws and tore a sizeable gash in the armored skin of the green dragon's back. The strike also caught Drago's arm, but Eldin's cloak managed to thwart any serious injury to the false Sentinel. His dragon wasn't nearly as lucky, and the talons ripped through the thick armor plating, causing it a great deal of pain, although not enough to bring it down.

Fox and Stormwise recovered from the dive just in time to watch as the dragon exploded from forest canopy and into clear air. They rotated out of their descent and resumed the chase. He knew they had caused some damage and hoped it would be enough to slow the beast down. A moment later they broke free of the canopy and emerged into the bright sunlight. Fox spied the dragon and watched as it continued to climb and head in a northerly direction toward darkening sky.

Drago pressed the dragon on. The young Sentinel and his bird had caused it some serious damage, but the wound wasn't fatal for the moment. Pushing the dragon forward, Drago observed the shifting and twisting clouds ahead of him and realized that his call had been heard. He looked back and saw the falcon emerge from the forest canopy but knew that the bird and the young elf wouldn't catch up before his surprise was on top of them.

Fox was so focused on his escaping mentor that he hardly noticed that the dark cloud in front of them was actually composed of dozens of dragons. By the time he realized his mistake, it was too late. The sky was a reptilian blur. Reds, blacks, browns, and greens--the sky was awash with them. The green dragon with Eldin on its back disappeared into the swarm, and Fox lost sight of them instantly… but at the moment that was the least of his worries.

The dragons raced toward Fox and Stormwise with rage in their eyes. The young elf pulled the reins back and to the left at the same time. Stormwise saw the beasts approaching and nearly panicked, but she responded to Fox's command, and they veered away from the onslaught. She banked hard toward one wing and turned, inverted for a moment before rotating to an upright position and diving in the direction of the trees. The dragons swarmed around them, and she was forced to twist and turn in every direction to avoid being torn to pieces.

The closest of the dragons crowded around Drago, protecting him and the green from their pursuers. They had responded to the ancient black dragon's call; his magic was old and beyond anything they dared resist. They could see right through the human shell he wore and recognized the soul of a dragon. Once they had surrounded and protected him, the horde turned on the falcon and its rider, turning the pursuer into the pursued.

Fox grabbed the pommel of Stormwise's saddle and clung to it for dear life. The giant falcon tucked in her wings and accelerated through the mass of encircling monsters. Nothing in the known world could dive faster than a falcon, and she managed to break free of the maelstrom of attacking beasts. She accelerated downward toward the Great Forest, heedless of the danger that diving into the trees could bring.

An instant later, just as Sentinel and falcon entered the protective canopy of trees, the sky rained acid and fire. The falcon zigged and zagged through the dense canopy, narrowly avoiding the larger branches before regaining control of the dive. The dragons' fire and acid rained over their heads but was contained by the massive leaves and branches of the upper canopy.

Once safe from the attack, they landed on a branch and looked up at the smoldering treetops. Fox's eyes burned and watered from the acidic smoke in the air, and he clenched his fists in frustration.

The black dragon had stolen Eldin's body and soul--now he had both Fox's friend and mentor *and* the key.

-Chapter Fifteen-

Enob

After the battle with the false Sentinel, Fox landed and debriefed the Captain of the Guard on the situation. The young Sentinel was furious with himself for allowing the key to be stolen and not being able to stop his mentor, although the elf guardsmen knew there was nothing more Fox could have done. They had witnessed most of the battle from their pursuit on the ground or close behind in the air, and they realized that what he did was far more than anyone else could even have attempted.

It was late in the evening when Fox returned to the Sentinels' Keep. His eyebrows had been singed slightly by the dragon fire, but for the most part he was not much worse for wear. There was nothing else he could do that evening. He had related everything about the chase to the Captain of the Guard, and it would now be up to him to report the situation to the King.

The Captain had tried to ease the young elf's mind, but he could not quash the anger boiling in his gut. As he returned Stormwise to the stables, Fox worked the chase over and over again mentally. He knew in his heart of hearts that Drago, the black dragon, had taken over Eldin's body, but he also had a keen awareness that his master was somehow still alive. ...He was determined to help rid him of the dragon's dark soul.

Finally he resigned himself to the situation at hand. He knew that what was done was done, so he turned his full attention to Stormwise for the moment. Fox examined her delicate wings meticulously, concerned that the fight might have torn open old wounds. Fortunately she had fared well and hadn't done any real damage to herself. He fed and watched over her a while longer, making sure she was comfortable in her stall before giving in to fatigue and dragging himself to his own quarters below.

The young elf followed a narrow set of steps from the stable down to the common room of the Sentinels' Keep. Waiting there for him to arrive was Enob, the King's High Wizard. Fox had half expected to find someone waiting for him to go over the events of the day and their next move, but he hadn't expected a wizard.

Enob watched Fox enter the room and gestured to him to take a seat on the couch across from him. Fox settled himself and looked up at the High Wizard. Enob wore a long, dark robe with a cowl hood that concealed most of his head from view and covered all but his hands and the tips of his leather boots.

"It seems the Dire Wolf King's prediction may be true," said Enob.

Fox had spoken of this briefly with the wizard weeks before when he, Stormwise, and Morwen had been rescued from the Nawg and transported safely back to Greylok. Fox had told Enob that before he had fallen unconscious from his wounds in the swamp, the King of the Dire Wolves had suggested that Eldin's body had been possessed by the black dragon. At the time Fox had been suffering from severe head trauma and could hardly stay conscious, let alone discuss at length the possibility that his friend and mentor had actually been possessed by an ancient reptile.

"Honestly I had hoped that the Dire Wolf King

was wrong, but deep down I knew it must be true. Why else would Eldin have disappeared and left the birds and me alone in the swamp?"

Enob agreed. "This is certainly true, considering the state in which we found you and the two birds. If it weren't for the dire wolves, you would probably not have left the swamp alive. The true Eldin would never have abandoned you, regardless of the circumstances."

Fox nodded and let Enob go on without commenting further. "I was deeply troubled by what had transpired in the swamp, and I wanted to look into the matter myself. I would have done so even more thoroughly and at greater length, but with the King's condition deteriorating so rapidly, it was necessary for me to stay with him as often as possible."

Fox nodded. "In all the commotion, I nearly forgot to ask about the King. How is he now? Is my uncle well? I had been planning to meet with him before I was called to the chase."

Enob smiled. "Yes, your uncle and the two IEA agents returned safely, and they brought with them more than just a single talon. The blood dragon herself helped them return. She provided a portion of one of her talons in return for information relating to an egg that was stolen from her. I was able to use the talon to create an elixir and administer it to the King. You'll be pleased to know that he is doing very well. He should be fully recovered in a few days."

Fox looked relieved. "That's great news! I'm so glad the King will be all right."

Enob nodded. "Yes, so am I… but that's not why I am here. As I was saying, I wanted to investigate further, so I allowed the healers to look after the King while I traveled to the swamp to locate the carcass of the black dragon. I needed to see for myself if what the dire wolf said was true. I was able to find the decomposing carcass of the beast easily enough. I conducted a few magical tests on the beast and came to the same conclusion. I can confirm what the dire wolf said: the body of the dead dragon was a discarded shell, and the soul of the beast has not left this plane of existence. I can only assume that our friend Eldin harbors the spirit of this creature, and I doubt that it is of his own free will."

The wizard paused for a second and gathered his thoughts. "Initially I was simply concerned for

Eldin's safety, but after the events that transpired today I must say that I'm even more deeply troubled. If my fears are justified and my suspicions are true, there is a crisis brewing that takes precedence even over our King's current state of health."

Enob's cowl shifted back ever so slightly, and Fox focused on the wizard's eyes. He saw the intense apprehension there and knew that the wizard meant what he was saying. "I realize that the beast in Eldin's form has stolen the key, and this situation is very serious, but please explain how this could be more critical than our King's health."

Enob looked at the young Sentinel for a moment and sighed. "As a Sentinel your first duty, above all else, is as guardian of the key."

Fox tried to reply, but Enob held up his hand and prevented him from speaking. "Over the centuries the key's purpose has faded from memory. Only a handful of people even know of its existence, and of those few an even smaller number know what it will unlock. Even the Sentinels who were charged with guarding it had long since forgotten its true purpose.

The Order of the Sentinels was first created to

guard the key and keep it safe at all costs, even if that meant sacrificing their lives to do so. Over the centuries the key was nearly forgotten, and the duties of the Sentinels changed. This is the reason why the number of Sentinels has declined over the ages, and it is why now only two individuals are tasked with the job--in this case, you and Eldin."

"I often wondered about that. Maybe that's why fewer and fewer people are born with the abilities Eldin and I seem to have," said Fox.

Enob smiled. "In the past many more had your gifts, and the number of Sentinels was significantly higher. The true reason for this is complex and difficult to understand, but it is essentially related to the key. Please don't misunderstand me--as long as the key exists, there will always be a Sentinel, but recently not as many have been needed. In some magical way, the universe was aware of this and balanced itself out. In the future your numbers may increase again… but let's hope that's not necessary."

Enob's expression darkened. "As a Sentinel, your primary duty is to guard the key--even with your life, if necessary. Eldin would have informed you about all this in due time... even though it was no longer foremost in his mind, and the need for individuals such as you two had declined. As the importance of the key was forgotten, so was the understanding of the danger of its falling into the wrong hands."

Fox shook his head, trying to take all of this in. "So what exactly does the key unlock?"

Enob smiled again. "Not tonight... the story is simply too long. Tomorrow we will travel to the city of Cloudview and seek out help to find Eldin. The Dire Wolf King was correct. A black dragon has possessed your mentor, and if what I have divined is true, then his captor is very, very old and dangerous. He *is* a creature by the name of Drago, and he is one of the very few that know the secret of the key and what it unlocks. Now it seems as though he is in possession of it, and I'm sure he's looking for a way to use it."

Enob stood, walked to the door, and hesitated at the threshold. He looked back at Fox and gestured to a small table in the corner of the room. "When you and the birds were found on the outskirts of the Cloudview after your ordeal in the swamp, you still had your pack with you. You neglected to mention that you had recovered the items necessary to fabricate your cloak, and hence, had completed your training."

He smiled at the young Sentinel. "Now get some rest… we leave at first light. I want to reach Cloudview as soon as possible. I'm not yet sure how, but I believe that the city is in some way relevant to this entire situation."

When Enob had left the room, Fox's eyes traveled to the table in the corner. For a long moment he sat still, gazing at the leather-wrapped parcel lying on its surface.

-Chapter Sixteen-

It's Elementary

The little red light on Kase's answering machine was blinking. The young agent stared at it for a few moments before his partner Murdox clamped onto his pant leg and dragged him out of the office. "No more… not tonight, at least. We're barely back from Greylok, we've been catching up with all the work here for days, it's nearly midnight, and I'm exhausted. I need to get some sleep, and so do you."

Kase looked down at Murdox. "All right already, but first thing in the morning we need to make a full report to the Commander about that demon-looking thing that we saw before we left for Greylok."

Murdox let go of the boy and looked up at him. "Yeah I agree… with everything else going on I nearly forgot. That thing scared the phooey out of me."

"Whatever that was, it crushed my gun with its bare hands and took off with the howler like it was

some kind of house cat." said Kase.

Murdox sniffed air in the hallway and sneezed. "Yeah, I think we're going to need to get that weapon replaced, but right now the only thing I care about is getting home and catching a few zees. We'll deal with everything else in the morning."

Commander Devin Crashblade watched from behind his desk as Kase and Murdox stumbled into his office the next day. "You two look exhausted. Sorry to have to drag both of you here on such short notice."

Kase plopped down on a well-worn leather chair while Murdox circled the floor beside him to find a comfortable spot.

"Sorry, Commander… we had a bit of a late night." Kase took a moment to gather his thoughts. "Before we get into new business… we already turned in a brief written report about this, but we need to make a full statement of the details that's rather overdue. When we were out chasing a howler before we left town to help the Elf King, we saw something strange--something that neither of us has ever seen before--and it nearly scared us to death."

Commander Crashblade looked down at Murdox, and the wolf-dog nodded in agreement. The Commander looked at his watch, sighed, and leaned back in his chair. "We've got a few minutes before our guests arrive. Tell me more about what you saw."

Just at that moment, the Commander's intercom buzzed. "Yes," he replied.

"Sir, your guests have arrived a bit early," a voice chimed out.

He looked over at Kase. "Sorry… we'll have to hear about it later."

Kase nodded without reply.

"Send them in," said the Commander.

Moment's later, two cloaked figures entered the room. The first was a fairly tall elf of approximately middle age, with unnaturally long white hair. It was Enob, the Elf King's wizard. He was wearing faded black robes and carried with him a satchel filled with dusty metal tubes. He had a stern expression on his face and looked very anxious to talk.

The second figure was also an elf but was considerably younger. He seemed in good physical shape and was about the same size as Kase, and like the young agent, appeared to be in early adolescence. His hair was dark and long, framing the delicately planed features common to most elves. The eyes set him apart, though; unlike others of his kind, his were gray. With one look at that keen gaze, the others realized instantly that this young elf was much more than he appeared.

The Commander rose from his chair and gestured to his visitors to take seats. "Thank you for coming. We don't get many elf visitors in the city, but when we do, I take them very seriously… especially wizards."

Enob placed his satchel on the floor next to Murdox and took a seat next to Kase. "It's nice to see you again, old friend. It's been quite some time since our paths crossed."

Crashblade nodded. "Yes, I believe it has been nearly eight years. It's a shame we can't get together under better circumstances." He looked over at Kase and Murdox. "I know you've already met my two agents here."

Enob nodded. "Yes, and both the King and I would like to express our thanks once again for their help."

"Good! Then I assume the King is recovering," said the Commander.

Enob grinned. "Yes, he is doing well. He's getting stronger every day. But please forgive my rudeness. I've forgotten to introduce my colleague. This is Fox. He's one of the King's Sentinels, and guardian to the King himself."

Murdox got up and walked over to the young Sentinel, and sniffed at his hand. "Hmm… I'll bet you're related to Asher."

Fox smiled and nodded and began scratching the wolf-dog behind the ears.

Kase watched in amazement as the young Sentinel won the wolf-dog over. "You *must* be related to Asher. You and he are the only two people I know who can get away with that and not get their hands snapped off."

Fox grinned. "Yes, Asher is my uncle. He apologizes for not being here, but his duties have kept him at the King's side… as would mine have done, were this not such urgent business on the King's behalf."

Enob glanced at the clock on the wall. "Yes, the

situation is critical, and I'm afraid we don't have much time for pleasantries," said the wizard.

Commander Crashblade sat back in his chair. "You sent word that Eldin has gone missing. I've worked with him in the past and know how capable he is--I don't even want to think about who or what could be responsible for his disappearance."

Enob looked at Fox, indicating it was time to retell his tale. The young Sentinel reiterated everything he could remember of the black dragon attack and the events that had taken place up to the present.

The agents of the Incantation Enforcement Agency listened to the story intently, and when Fox had finished, they all sat in silence for a moment. Finally Murdox shook his head from side to side. "Oh, great... now I know why you wanted to get us involved. Black dragon possession sounds right up the alley of the Counter Curse Division." The wolf-dog looked at Commander Crashblade. "You do realize that would be sarcasm, of course."

The Commander didn't bother to respond to Murdox's snide remark but instead looked over at Enob. "You mentioned the Gold Trust Raid when we spoke earlier. How does this relate to Fox's story?"

Enob leaned slightly forward, trying to get more comfortable in his seat. "Yes, of course. I read in your daily paper that not long ago the Gold Trust Bank was broken into by what appeared to be a band of organized ogres and trolls. Fortunately it also mentioned that the robbery was foiled before anything was stolen. Is this true?"

Crashblade glanced at Kase and Murdox. "Yes. Actually, these two agents handled that situation just prior to their assignment involving your King. They managed to locate a series of steam tunnels that ran beneath the bank. An organized band of ogres was using the battle overhead to cover their tracks and sneak into the bank undetected. If not for the fine job these two did, they probably would have gotten away with even more than they did."

Kase and Murdox looked up at Crashblade and spoke in unison. "*...even more than they did?*"

Crashblade pulled a file from his desk and opened it. "Yes, I hadn't had a chance to inform you yet, but I'm sorry to say that the bank's vault was actually broken into the same night that the raid took place. It took nearly a week for anyone to realize anything was stolen, but a particularly observant bank employee found that one of the safety deposit boxes had been tampered with, and the lock was broken. At that point, the bank called us in, and we reviewed the security tapes in greater detail."

The Commander looked down at the file and skimmed through the information quickly, trying to put words to the strange event. "The odd thing is that we weren't able to identify the thief from the video. All we could see was a distorted image, almost a blur that shifted from place to place within the room. It stopped at the box in question, and the next thing you know the locked popped open and a long cylindrical tube was pulled out. The tube was swallowed in the distortion, and the whole thing was over in a few seconds."

Enob and Fox looked at each other for a brief moment. Commander Crashblade watched their reactions for a moment and then continued. "I'm speculating that the whole incident, even the events with the ogres in the steam tunnels, was nothing more than an elaborate diversionary scheme to cover this crime. The perpetrator in question must somehow have gotten his hands on some kind of invisibility cloak and used it to sneak into the bank."

"Yes, I believe you're right," said Enob, "but I doubt that the ogres would ever have gone along with such a plan. They were most probably tricked, as well, and convinced that the battle ruse would work--they probably knew nothing of the actual crime. I doubt they were interested in anything but the gold."

Crashblade nodded. "Yes, I agree. I don't think that ogres would have had any understanding of what was stolen, or any desire to obtain it. The mastermind behind this crime wanted only what was in that safety deposit box. From the outcome, it seems likely that he cared little for the gold. If the plan had worked--and it very nearly did--then the ogres would have stolen the gold, too. Either way, it would have worked out for the thief… and at the end of the day, he still got away with what he was after."

Enob looked over at Fox and nodded ever so slightly. "Commander, can you tell me what was taken from that vault?"

The Commander watched the young Sentinel as he removed his travel cloak and placed it on the back of his chair. He than reached for his backpack, which he had placed on the floor when he first arrived.

Crashblade thought about the question for a moment and then proceeded. "After reviewing the surveillance video, we pinpointed the box in question and traced it to the owner. Strangely enough, it belonged to an old dwarf king. I had a few detectives try to locate him, but apparently he had died rather suddenly a week or so prior to the theft.... The whole thing sounded fishy to me, so we dug a little deeper and located his closest living relatives, but no one had knowledge of the safe deposit box in question... nor was it ever officially willed to any heirs."

Murdox had been busy scratching an itch behind his ear with a hind paw, but he stopped and looked up at Commander Crashblade. "You said 'officially.' What about unofficially?"

Crashblade smiled. "I thought you might pick up on that. You're right. Officially it was never willed to any heir, but my detectives pushed a little harder. It actually didn't take much more than a few telephone calls back to the office to uncover some of the family skeletons. A couple dozen unpaid parking tickets, an illegal mining claim, and an overlooked shoplifting incident later... and the heir in question spilled the beans."

Crashblade stopped and looked over at the chair in which Fox had been sitting just a moment earlier. The young elf had simply vanished from sight. Then for a split second the chair looked fuzzy, shifting slightly out of focus until the distortion cleared a few moments later.

Fox slid the cowl of his cloak back onto his shoulders, and his head emerged from the distortion. "I assume this is what you saw on the surveillance video?"

Crashblade nodded.

"The cloak I'm wearing gives me the ability to blend into my surroundings almost instantly. True invisibility does not exist, but the cloak has the ability to mimic or reflect what is surrounding and behind it. If I remain perfectly still, I will effectively disappear, but if I move you will see a distorted image until the cloak catches up and matches the background...."

Crashblade nodded his head up and down several times. "Yes, that is exactly what I saw, and that answers a lot of questions."

Enob and Fox looked at each other for a moment before the wizard spoke. "Please finish. You were about to say what the heir had told you."

"Yes, of course… where was I? Oh, yes… the heir spilled the beans and told us that his great uncle, King Chiselright, had been a collector of rare artifacts, and in particular, rare maps. Apparently the contents of this safe deposit box was nearly one of a kind, as well as one of his most prized possessions. Only one other such map existed in the world, and that was the original."

Enob and Fox exchanged glances again as Crashblade went on. "The detectives pressed, and the heir related what he knew of its history. Apparently the original had been copied eons ago, but the copy's existence had remained secret. The original map belonged to the Elf Kingdom and was supposed to be the only one ever made. The story goes that even the forger who created the copy had been killed to keep the inscriptions a secret."

All eyes were on the Commander, encouraging him to continue.

"Yes, well, the heir knew very little else. He

never actually got to see it. He knew only that the map depicted the land on which this very city was built and that it contained a rendering of the original foundation, before the city was constructed."

Enob's frown deepened, and he removed a metal tube from his satchel. "What I most feared has come to pass. The black dragon, Drago, has both the key and the knowledge of where to find the lock that it opens."

The wizard rose from his chair, his robes rustling across the floor as he went to a small table at the back of the room. He removed an ancient map from the tube and carefully unfurled its ragged edges, spreading it out on the table for all to see. "There is little question that Eldin has been possessed, and if what we know is true, he now goes by the name of Drago. Without question, we couldn't have picked a more dangerous enemy."

Commander Crashblade looked up from the map for a moment. "Are we sure it's Eldin who has been possessed by Drago?"

Both Enob and Fox nodded in response. "There is little doubt of this," said Enob.

"I got close enough to the thief to verify his

identity," said the young Sentinel. "He's been my mentor for nearly ten years, and I'm sure it was Eldin."

Enob turned his attention back to the ancient map. "Both the key and this map are useless to anybody but one who knows their secret. Only the King and I know the entire story behind the key's true purpose."

"If that's so," said Kase, "how is it that this dragon knows what they're for?"

Enob looked up for a moment. "This also crossed my mind, so I traveled to the swamp and performed an ancient magical ritual on the carcass of the fallen dragon. With great effort I confirmed what the Dire Wolf King had said."

Kase stepped away from the table for a moment, grabbed his backpack, and opened it. After a few moments of digging, he pulled out a large, weathered field guide with a faded image of a gold dragon on the cover. He flipped through the pages and pointed to an image of a black dragon about a quarter of the way through the book.

"Is this the dragon you saw?" asked the young agent.

Murdox pushed his nose into the book and read

a snippet of the text below the picture. "Yep, it gives a good number of details here about accurately identifying individual dragons. There don't seem to be many of the ancient black ones left. Oh, and look here… it names the living black ones individually, with biographical data for the purpose of identification." He looked up at Enob. "I hope that ritual of yours wasn't *too* dangerous. All you really needed was this book."

Enob bristled. "Yes, well… I prefer the old ways, however dangerous they might be. Anyone can read a book… but as I was saying, Drago is one of the oldest of his kind. He could very well have been aware of the key and its use, but it required possessing Eldin's memories to gain the knowledge of the key's whereabouts and how to acquire it."

Fox and Kase were now both looking at the book. "This really does give a lot of detail about Drago," said Kase. "Did you know he was one of the very first dragons of his kind and that his mother was actually thought to be a demon? Oh, I didn't know this. It says that dragons as a species are very inquisitive and that, to them, possessing knowledge is almost as important as hoarding treasure."

Enob rolled his eyes. "Yes, I get the point. I'll get the book… but that does offer up another piece of useful information. It probably explains how he learned of this second map, although I doubt I will ever determine precisely how he discovered its existence, for even I knew nothing of it… and I am the guardian of the original." The wizard hesitated for a moment. "I suppose that, just as your book says, he sought out such knowledge and must have stored it away until it became of use to him. Over the ages Drago must have discovered numerous pieces to the puzzle, but with patience and perseverance he held onto them until he could put them all together. Eldin was probably the final piece of the puzzle, and with his knowledge it all came together."

Murdox was shaking his head. "So, what exactly are you trying to say?"

Enob looked down at his feet for a second. "Drago is a master of sinister dragon magic, and now with Eldin's body and mind, he also has the skills of an elf Sentinel. However, all this is nothing compared with the damage he could do if he uses the key."

-Chapter Seventeen-

The Age of Doom

Enob stood at the table looking down at the ancient map. "This map was created ages ago, during the building of this city. Alone, the map is of little significance, but to one who knows the story I am about to tell, it is of great importance."

The map depicted a small portion of the surrounding countryside and what looked like an architectural drawing of a huge building's foundation. Near the center of the foundation was drawn in red a strange sigil.

Enob pointed to this mark and shook his head. "Why, I cannot explain, but this mark represents the entrance to one of the greatest secrets of all time. This spot marks the entrance to a vast cavern that hides a hidden vault, which only the key that Drago now possesses will open. The vault is sealed behind an impregnable magic door… by no means can the door be opened with anything other than that key. Within the vault is an artifact of unsurpassed power."

The wizard looked very tired at that moment, as if he were struggling with an inner turmoil that was about to devour him. "What I am going to tell you is a tale that only a few have ever heard. The mere mention of this tale will begin a cosmic chain of events that I have no knowledge of how to control… but to keep Drago from what he might discover, I must tell it to all of you."

Enob stood silently for a moment and then began his tale. "It was the Age of Doom. Long ago, deep underground, a dark wizard had found what had once been hidden. Etched upon a stone tablet was a single word. The word, the one True Wyrd, was the key to ultimate power, and this Wyrd was then spoken. A long-forgotten prophecy had finally come to pass, and man was on the verge of extinction.

"Originally, eons before that, the Builder of the world had used the magic of the Wyrd to fabricate the very foundation of the planet, and with this power he built a world. Once finished, he feared what would become of his creation if this Wyrd were to be spoken by the wrong individual. Wisely he took the carved tablet and hid it deep in the mountains, where he believed it would never be found.

"In time the Builder left the world. As was for the best, the tablet's location was lost, and its history was mostly forgotten. Civilizations grew and fell as time ticked on. Thousands of years passed, and through countless generations, fragments of the world's beginning became myth and speculation.

"But the true story was not entirely lost. Magic had grown strong in the world. Wizards began to control the elements and the environment. The wizards grew powerful, far stronger than the world had ever seen. Their might was unquestioned. In their struggle to gain more power, they discovered the long-forgotten tale of the Wyrd, and tirelessly they sought to find the tablet.

"Eventually the stone was found. A dark wizard spoke the Wyrd and used it for evil purposes, and darkness fell over the world.

"As the Builder had feared, the Wyrd brought forth deceit and corruption. Unchecked power flowed from the one who spoke the Wyrd. He brought the planet to its knees. No one dared challenge the might of this dark wizard. For more than three hundred years, he ruled with an iron fist, but even this success could not quench his thirst for power. In his lust for ultimate control of the world, he decided to strike a final blow to his enemies. With his magic he created armies of fierce, heartless creatures. With these new forces, he intended to rid the world once and for all of those who opposed him.

"The fair kingdoms of the world were under siege. The last hope for victory brought the battle to the foothills of the dark wizard's stronghold. In the shadow of his fortress, defended by beasts bred in the deepest pits of doom, the armies of the world were driven back. All seemed lost, for the horde of the dark wizard had rained destruction and death upon his foes.

"Swarming armies of wicked, swine-like creatures waged total war, but all was not lost, for the putrid beasts were weak and had little intelligence. Even in their great numbers, they could still be defeated and driven back... but the dark wizard had far more lethal allies in the ax-bearing ogres and club-wielding trolls that he held in thrall with his magic.

"Mass upon mass, legion upon legion of the porcine beasts would be sent to soften his enemy. The ogres and the trolls would then join the fray with their steel axes and twisted wooden clubs. Days led to weeks as these fierce battles progressed to their deadly outcome. The land was devastated in the wake of the war, with great black carrion birds slowly circling the battlefields, fat from no shortage of meals.

"The dark wizard felt certain the end of the battle was at hand. From his lofty view high in the stony tower of his fortress, he watched the horrifying war unfold; knowing that soon it would be over and he would be victorious. Even though armies of his vile soldiers lay fallen ten-to-one next to his enemy, he could still envision victory, for the dark wizard still commanded hordes of foul creatures that he could use to strike the final blow. His enemy had shown great cunning and valor, but the armies of the free world had dwindled almost to the point of extinction.

"Smug with presumed victory, the dark wizard decided to send his most fearsome creation into battle, for he wished to wreak dread and despair across what remained of his enemy's forces. From that day onward--for this was the first time that these creatures had been glimpsed--they were known as the nargoyles. Always cloaked, these winged specters wrought terror in whoever met their hate-filled gaze. Creatures of living stone and shadow, some twisted cross between a gargoyle and a phantasm, in history little is known of how they came into existence. They were thought once to have been slaves of the dark wizard, poisoned by his wickedness until they had become transformed into grim fiends. They would perch motionlessly in a ring surrounding the upper tower of their master's fortress. High upon the dark walls, they would wait patiently for the moment when they could rain fear from the sky.

"That moment came, and the dark wizard sent out all of his nargoyles that day. The beasts soared on bat-like wings from the high tower walls. They clutched great wooden staves, and the afternoon sun gleamed off wicked, silver-pronged spearheads. Without mercy or remorse, they dove into the ranks of the enemy, slashing away any hope of victory. Mortal weapons merely irritated their spectral hides, and the armies of the world soon learned that *nargoyle* was another name for fear.

"Strangely, this maneuver became the turning point of the battle, but not in the way it had been anticipated. Unbeknownst to the dark wizard, a lone warrior was, with great stealth, threading her way to the tower. She carried a black arrow of awesome power. This would be the best and final hope of all the free races. The blade of this arrow had been wrought in a blaze of dragon fire from the rarest of metals. Its wooden shaft had been carved from the branch of the eldest of the black oaks. Laid upon this shaft were the tail feathers of a true nighthawk, a bird thought even by the sylvan elves of the Deep Woods to be extinct.

"The completed arrow had been brought to an ancient ring of stones that lay hidden upon a remote island deep within the cold, storm-ridden waters of the Northern Sea. Here a council comprised of the races of men, elves, dwarves, and fairies had met. They gathered their power and channeled their strength into the weapon. But even this they feared would not be enough to waylay the power of the speaker of the Wyrd.

"At that time, knowing what truly must be

sacrificed, an old and wise wizard of men gave his life for the creation of the arrow. His name was Fairhope, and through the power of his sacrifice, the arrow could bind the condemned and forever hold him between worlds, where his evil strength would be rendered useless.

"At that point the arrow traveled into the hands of the elves of the Deep Wood, for they amongst all the races were best known for their skill with a bow. A champion among them was chosen, and she led a small, secretive quest to slay their enemy. In the end she was all that remained of her group. Each of them had in some way or another fallen so that she could complete the mission.

"Wearing the filthy armor and rags of her enemy, she snuck into the dark wizard's tower. Through great skill she remained undetected and reached the uppermost level where the Evil One resided. Even though she had been mortally wounded by her passage through the bloody war that raged below, her sheer determination drove her on. She knew that one of them would soon be dead.

"More than just luck was with the elf woman

that day. The dark wizard had sent all of his minions to finish off his enemies, and his attention was drawn to the field of battle. He did not detect her presence until it was too late. This elf warrior, brave beyond all measure, made her way into her enemy's presence and released the arrow of his doom.

"The speaker of the Wyrd fell at her feet, his mortal body defeated by a single arrow. When his evil spirit attempted to escape the mortal world, spectral hands reached out from the netherworld and bound the soul of the dark wizard. The phantom howled in defiance, tearing invisible scars into the stone floor of the keep as it was dragged between worlds to be held captive for all eternity.

"The elf warrior Amrael, no longer bound to her quest, fell to her knees and died a heroine a moment later. Only through this tale are her and the wizard Fairhope's sacrifices remembered, for as I said this tale remains a closely guarded secret. But their legacy continued, for after her the Sentinels were created, and later the Wizard's Council was established in memory of Fairhope.

"When the dark wizard fell, his armies, no

longer held in thrall by his power, grew weak and cowardly. The armies of man and elf, even in what few numbers were left, easily overcame the ghastly horde and dispatched the few who did not run from the field of battle. What remained of the swine-like creatures were allowed to slink back into the filthy holes in the ground from which they had crept. Less compassion was shown to the hobgoblins and ogres and their kind, for they had been willing allies of the dark wizard.

"So the armies of man, renewed in strength, brought down the remainder of the horde. They destroyed their war engines and freed the enslaved beasts of burden that had hauled them. What remained of the Evil One's army scattered into small bands and disappeared into the far corners of the world.

"With the dark wizard's demise, the nargoyles became susceptible to mortal weapons. Five of the loathsome beasts fell, but the sixth--the leader of their kind--withdrew from battle and disappeared.

"Later it was learned that he had returned to the dark wizard's keep. There he collected the tablet on which the Wyrd was inscribed and was witnessed soaring from the tower of his fallen master. From this point little is known, but his trail was picked up far across the deep blue western ocean. There the nargoyle must have climbed the moss-ridden steps of the ancient temple that had once stood below what is now Cloudview. Amongst the fallen stone pillars that littered the floor of this ancient structure, he found an entrance to a vast cave system.

"Elven trackers finally hunted him down and trapped him within the very caves where he had sought refuge, but in the end they never brought him out. The nargoyle was a twisted creation of magic and not wholly of this world, and because of this he was unable to use the power of the Wyrd. He eventually relinquished the tablet without a struggle and allowed the most powerful wizards of the time to hide it away from the world. Using strong magic, they created a chamber to store the tablet and seal it with a lock that had only one key. When the final ceremonies had been performed, the nargoyle slipped away from the trackers, and using his gargoyle heritage, changed himself into stone and disappeared amongst the rock to remain as guardian over the ages.

"Centuries passed. Peace reigned across the free

world. Men and elves rebuilt their cities and grew in power. The races separated of their own free will and segregated themselves within their own territories. Men built vast cities along the western coastlines and deep onto the plains of the inner continents. The elves took to the forests of the world and shaped their kingdoms within the numberless trees. The dwarves strove to dig ever deeper into the mountains and carve massive stone fortresses in search of their precious rare metals. For more than three centuries, evil was driven from the lives of men."

He looked at each of them and added, "But it seems the dark clouds are once more gathering on the horizon."

They all sat in silence for a moment, digesting what Enob had said. Finally Kase found the nerve to speak. "What if I told you that I think we saw a nargoyle before we left Cloudview for Greylok?"

Enob looked over at the young agent. "Are you sure?"

Murdox looked up at the wizard. "What we saw was like nothing we've ever seen before."

Enob looked even more agitated than before. "If

this is true, then the guardian has already been awakened. The entrance to the cavern must have crumbled. I doubt Drago has found it yet, but he must be close."

Murdox looked at Kase. "For weeks now the howlers have been agitated--even more than usual. I'll bet this creature has been snacking on them."

Kase nodded. "That answers a few questions. I've been wondering why the howler attacks have increased. They're mad. That beast must have been around for a while." The boy looked to Enob. "If Drago has yet to find the cave, what do you think woke it?"

Enob pondered the question for a moment and looked at Fox. "It's impossible to say, but for every check there is a balance in the universe--light and shadow, good and bad. The Wyrd is beyond any power we can comprehend. Principally because the Wyrd had long been forgotten and the key had remained hidden, only two Sentinels were needed to protect the secret. Perhaps the creature's awakening is the universe's way of balancing the Sentinels' charge to protect the key. The nargoyle was not guarding the Wyrd from being found at all, but rather a creation of evil to protect it until its master returned... or a suitable one took his place. In this case I dare say the guardian has found a new master."

Enob quickly rolled up the map and placed it back in the tube. "We have no time to waste. If the nargoyle is awake, the Wyrd is in danger of being found. The cavern must be open. If Drago enters it, only the lock stands in his way... and he now has the key.

-Chapter Eighteen-

Deep Below the City

The small party composed of Kase, Murdox, Enob, and Fox exited the V train as it made its final stop. They had reached the very lowest level of the metropolis and disembarked on a platform where few dared venture. The platform was deserted, and no one else exited the train after them. A moment later the pistons of the gleaming steam engine hissed and whined behind them, and the train pulled away from the platform in a cloud of billowing smoke that drifted over their heads.

Murdox watched the train disappear down the tunnel, accelerating into a vertical position until the final car vanished as it climbed upwards on its journey back into the city, proper. "So much for a quick ride home," said the wolf-dog.

The city of Cloudview was an enormous structure, more precisely many cities in one. The entire metropolis was more than a hundred levels tall and still climbing, and each level was a city in itself. The horizon was composed of towers, cathedrals, and spires, each in competition to drive ever higher into the sky. The tallest of the immense skyscrapers on each of the city's levels reached high into the sky and acted as columns designed to support the next level of the overall structure.

Visible between the countless buildings, the skyline was alive with glittering lights and rivers of traffic. At times the sound of traffic was so intense that it could have been mistaken for a beehive, with vehicles buzzing about the city in controlled mayhem.

Even the weather had been manipulated to suit the needs of the population, and each city generated its own system through a complicated and magically enhanced weather-creating device. For some unknown reason, though, it always seemed just as unpredictable as the real thing.

The machine also created such a perfect rendering of an artificial sky that both flying creatures and flying vehicles had a difficult time determining where the actual sky ended and each city's ceiling began. Needless to say, this uncertainty could cause quite a traffic hazard.

Beneath the shimmering sprawl of the structure, however, another world existed, and the little group of travelers found themselves well below ground--deep in the bowels of Cloudview. The lower levels were set in dark shadows, places where the sun never shined and danger lurked in every corner.

The city above denied the existence of this sinister substrate, and few but the most daring of adventurers traveled into its midst. Here the dark sky was lit only by artificial means, and even the weather machine that worked so efficiently to create seasons in the world above had given up on this domain, leaving the inhabitants in a perpetual winter.

Few dared venture into these parts, as the residents were not of a respectable sort. These were the villains and scoundrels, the thieves and felons of the world above, but down below they were just the locals. They were proud to be the dregs of society. The law of the land had given up on this place, and the locals created their own society… one where survival of the fittest was law.

The little group of travelers steadied themselves against a brisk breeze that blew a cloud of snow in their faces.

"From what I know of the inhabitants, this weather probably suits them," said Murdox.

In the distance an eerie howl brought them to attention, and they hastened off the platform. According to a decrepit overhead sign, they were in the Kelson Point district. The ancient map Enob had brought along was far too old to reference towns or streets. They could use it only as a topographical guide to set them in the general direction of where the entrance to the caverns might be hidden.

"According to the story of the Wyrd, the nargoyle brought the tablet to an ancient stone temple," said Kase.

Enob nodded. "Yes, that's where we need to go, but I doubt the structure still stands. We'll need to find someone who can point us in the right direction."

Murdox sniffed at the air. "I think I have an idea where we can find someone."

The wolf-dog looked up at Kase for a moment. "Your father and I came down here a few times, tracking down leads. I know a bartender who just might help us out."

They headed down Canal Street for a time, letting Murdox lead the way, and then turned to follow the canal itself. The dog wound his way through a few back streets and eventually emerged in a filthy alley not far from what they learned was Highland Point. The wolf-dog stopped about halfway down the alley, under the light of a dim street lamp. The wind began to howl overhead, and a line of sinister-looking clouds drifted in from just over the artificial horizon.

"Great! This just gets better and better," said the wolf-dog as he snuffled at the sky. "It looks like a storm is brewing."

Right on cue, thunder clapped overhead, and a bolt of lightening leaped across the dark sky. They bundled up against the cold and headed deeper into the alley. The others followed Murdox as he led them between two abandoned buildings and back to the edge of the canal, adjacent to a rickety bridge that crossed over it.

The wolf-dog looked up at the rest of the little party. "See I told you I'd get you there."

No one spoke, but Enob did raise his eyebrow ever so slightly.

"Don't worry. We don't have to cross the bridge... the bar is under it." Murdox turned and glared at the little group. "Come on, you sissies, it's about as safe as we can get around here. What better place to get information than a seedy bar?"

The little company cast one final glance at the bridge and walked to the edge of the canal. They found a narrow set of stairs that led them down to a slippery cobblestone deck a few feet over the dirty water. The group treaded lightly on the green-slime-coated stones and stopped in front of a weathered wooden door set at the edge of the bridge's foundation.

Two oil-burning lamps illuminated an ancient sign just over the doorframe. The paint had mostly flaked off, but they could still make out *Wolf's Den* stenciled onto the splintered wood.

Kase watched as a curl of gray smoke drifted up from one of the lamps. "Here goes nothing!"

Enob nodded, grabbed hold of the iron handle that was suitably fashioned in the shape of a growling wolf's head, and pushed open the door. It swung open, and a pool of red light spilled into the entryway. The little group stood in the entrance for a moment, letting their eyes adjust to the strange light.

The air inside the bar was smoky, and their ears pounded from a wave of loud music reverberating off the walls in an unrelenting beat. Strobe lights pulsed through the hazy atmosphere, while laser lights drew complex shapes on the walls and ceilings in an intensely colorful kaleidoscopic pattern.

The place was packed with a collection of every nightmarish creature imaginable. Ghouls, ogres, harpies, hags, even congealed slime-like creatures gyrated and danced to the relentless beat.

Kase looked over at Fox. "Talk about culture shock!"

Fox looked back and yelled. "What did you say?"

"I said *talk about culture shock,*" replied Kase at just below a yell.

Fox smirked and nodded in response.

The place was big--a lot bigger than it looked from the outside. The group pushed past the doorway and wove through the crowd in the direction of the bar.

A few eyes turned toward them, but most of the patrons took little notice.

The counter of the bar was long, stretching most of the way across the room. It was made of a dark red wood that had been polished to a brilliant sheen, and numerous barstools lined the length of it. Unfortunately most of the stools were occupied, so the little group was forced to slip into a narrow slot between a wretched old hag and a horrid-smelling ghoul.

The ghoul took one look at Murdox and licked its chops. It inched its way closer to the wolf-dog and casually began sniffing at him. Murdox pushed a little closer to Kase so as not to start any trouble, but the nasty creature followed right after him.

According to Kase's *Great Big Anthology of Annoying Creatures,* ghouls were just about the foulest beasts to walk the planet. They appeared to be more or less humanoid but with mottled, decaying flesh drawn tight across partially visible bones. They had beady little eyes and greasy black hair that was typically infested with crawling insects. Most wore rotted skins that came from some poor creature that they had recently eaten.

Murdox bumped into Kase as he tried to push farther away from the stinking creature.

"Hey, watch it!" Kase complained. "There's not enough room in here as it is."

Murdox gulped out loud and gestured with his head toward the foul creature that was just about to take a bite out of his rear end. Before Kase had a chance to do anything about it, Fox intervened. Without a sound he had managed to slip between Murdox and the ghoul.

Kase watched in amazement. One moment the ghoul was about to take a bite out of the wolf-dog, and the next moment it was yelping and pushing itself away from the bar.

"You're pretty handy, aren't you?" said Kase, impressed.

Fox just smiled and scratched Murdox behind the ears.

A couple of minutes later, a satyr appeared behind the bar. He pulled a rag from around his waste and wiped the surface in front of them. He growled gruffly, then coughed and cleared his throat. "Terribly sorry about the ghoul. I usually don't condone that type of behavior in my establishment."

He looked at the little group for a moment and shook his head. "No, you can't let your customers eat other customers… it's just not good for business. We don't get topsiders around here too often, and you've stirred up quite a commotion. Anyway, first round's on the house."

Enob looked around the room and noticed quite a few eyes focused on their little group. "I'm afraid we're in a bit of a hurry. Could we trade the drinks for some information?"

The satyr watched Enob for a few seconds. "Suit yourself. What kind of info are you looking for?"

"We're looking for the ruins of an ancient temple that stood somewhere near the city center area. It's probably been long since built over, but maybe a plaque or memorial was erected where it once stood…."

The satyr unconsciously continued to wipe the bar while he thought about it. "Yeah, I think I have seen something like that."

A fight suddenly broke out in the middle of the dance floor, and the music ground to a halt. The satyr's ears perked up, and he grabbed a huge spiked mace from behind the bar. In a single leap, he bounded over the counter and landed just at the far side of Enob. He leaned in for a parting word. "I believe what you're looking for was built over for a railway station ages ago, but even that was long since replaced with a newer one. That station still stands, and you'll find a small memorial to the temple in what was the main thoroughfare."

The fight on the dance floor was getting louder, and the entire crowd was beginning to get riled. "It's easy to find… just follow the canal, and you'll run right into it. Now, if you'll excuse me…," said the satyr as he dashed into the crowd with his mace held high.

The small party left the bar behind and climbed back up to street level. They followed the canal deeper into the city, as the satyr had instructed. The storm seemed to have gotten a lot closer, and snow was already beginning to fall. They walked past filthy industrial complexes marred with graffiti and gang-related symbols. Black soot from long-abandoned refineries quickly turned the snow gray as it hit the grimy brick walls of the buildings on its way to the ground.

Seemingly abandoned buildings loomed overhead. Most of their windows were boarded up or blackened, but now and again the foursome would catch a glimpse of movement, and they knew the under-city was anything but abandoned. This gave them a very uneasy feeling as they walked through poorly lit alleys, afraid that unseen eyes were watching every move they made as they traveled ever deeper into the slums.

It was cold and miserable, but they knew that the foul weather was probably what was keeping them from being visited by any number of unwanted guests. Even so, they paid particular attention to their surroundings as they traveled, and eventually they made it to a rusted fence surrounding an antiquated Horizontal Train station, more commonly known as an HT. All the levels had similar transportation systems for city commuting. The V train provided vertical transport between various levels of Cloudview, while the HT moved passengers horizontally on a single level. These usually radiated outward from the city center, as this one once had, but like the rest of the lower level it must have fallen into disrepair and eventually been abandoned altogether.

The building was old and decaying, and the ancient brick-and-mortar walls looked as though they could collapse at any time. The little group stood at the fence and shook their heads, and of course Murdox was the first to speak. "Why do we always get stuck going into old rundown rat's nests like this? Can't the bad guys ever go to a nice tropical island or at least a fancy hotel?" the irritated wolf-dog demanded.

Occupied with the lock on the gate, Kase ignored his partner. "This looks like the place that the bartender mentioned, but this lock hasn't been tampered with. Do you suppose we got here before Drago?"

Murdox snuffled at the fence. "Nope… I think he was already here."

Fox studied the ground. "It looks like he's been here, and then his tracks go off again in a different direction. I'll bet he found another way in… one that might not generate too much attention from the locals."

"Hold on… I've got just the thing." Kase pulled his backpack from his back and unzipped the flap.

A minute or so later, after digging through the

contents of his magical pack, the young agent removed a large bolt cutter and easily snapped the clasp off the lock. "I thought this would come in handy after our little incident in the steam tunnels under the Gold Trust Bank," Kase told Murdox, who nodded in agreement.

Fox raised his eyebrows. "Looks like you can be pretty handy, yourself."

They cautiously made their way to the front of the building, and it was clear that it was probably quite impressive at one time. Now it looked like nothing more than a rundown haven for vagrants and scoundrels.

The interior was pitch black, so Kase grabbed flashlights from his pack, handing one to each of the elves. They scanned the interior of the room and found that they were standing in the main thoroughfare. Their lights reflected on marble flooring that was once smooth and polished but had become cracked and broken in countless places. When their lights shone on the walls and ceilings, they found them to be in an even worse state. A quick investigation revealed huge, gaping holes in the walls and multiple debris piles from a crumbling ceiling that looked like it could collapse onto their heads at any moment.

They followed the main hall deeper into the building until Murdox stopped them in their tracks.

"Shhh… I hear voices coming from down the hall!"

Fox whispered to the group, "I hear them too. We had better turn off the flashlights. I'll put on my chameleon cloak and move on ahead to investigate."

They all agreed and extinguished their lights, leaving them momentarily blinded. Their eyes adjusted quickly to the darkness until they could see a dim glow coming from the direction of the voices. Fox had already slipped away, so the rest of the group waited in the darkness for his return.

A couple of minutes passed, and the young Sentinel came back with news. "About fifty meters down the hall, the tunnel gives way to what looks like the main train platform. Numerous metal walkways extend all the way around a large room and converge in a giant spiraling ramp that leads to the ground. On each level, signs point to tunnels that lead away from the ramp to what I assume were once different train platforms. The tunnel we're in is about midway up the ramp. The good news is that it looks like the ground level has collapsed, revealing a dark pit that drops off farther than I can see."

"That sounds like great news!" said Kase. "I'll bet they built this station right over the cave we're looking for, and the floor probably fell into the cave's entrance."

Fox nodded his head vigorously. "Yes, that's what I'm thinking."

"So what's the bad news?" asked Murdox.

Fox hesitated for a second. "The bad news is that we have to get past three thugs carrying spiked clubs, and what I suppose is a nargoyle, to get to the pit."

-Chapter Nineteen-

Distraction

The small company stood in the dimly lit abandoned railway station. They concealed themselves amid the shadows of a large spiraling ramp that ran along the outer walls of the station's main concourse. At the base of the ramp, about three floors down, was an entrance to a vast cavern system that concealed a hidden vault, which both they and Drago now sought.

The station area was illuminated by a few overhead bulbs that provided barely enough light to see anything. All around them were numerous tunnels that had at one time led passengers to various train platforms for commuting around this city level. Directly behind them were the main terminal hall and the way out, and below them was a collapsed floor that had fallen into the cave's entrance. To their great dismay, guarding the entrance were three hefty orc henchmen wielding spiked clubs… and what was most certainly the nargoyle that Kase and Murdox had seen before.

This had become the kind of game Fox understood best, and he quickly took control of the situation. "I'll distract the nargoyle and draw him away from the cave." He looked at the little group for a moment. "Do you think you can handle the remaining three guards?"

Without hesitation Kase drew his new Berrington Model 13 pistol and held it up for all to see.

Murdox whimpered a little in the background but was kind enough to keep his snoot shut.

"I'll do what I can to help," said Enob.

Fox retrieved a long ash bow and a quiver of arrows that had been concealed beneath his cloak and handed them to Enob. Even in the poor light, everyone spotted the black-shafted arrow with the trio of dark tail feathers amongst the others in the quiver.

"If your story holds true, wizard, this nargoyle may be more than a match for me," said Fox. "The best I can do is to keep him occupied while you three get into the cave and stop Drago… at any cost." The young

Sentinel looked into the darkness of the cave for a second. "I'll do what I can to find you in time before the real excitement begins. Just leave a trail for me to follow so I can locate you when the time comes."

Fox pulled his sword from its sheath and lifted the cowl of his cloak back over his head until he completely disappeared from view. He slipped away silently from the group and vanished into the shadows.

Less than a minute later, the nargoyle howled in pain and separated itself from the three henchmen. Enob, Kase, and Murdox used the distraction wisely and charged down the platform toward the remaining three guards. Distracted by the fight the nargoyle was having with a seemingly invisible foe, the three guards hardly noticed the others approaching. The distraction had lasted only a few seconds when Kase gave away their position by trying to shoot the largest one of the group with his pistol. His aim hadn't gotten any better, and he only managed to fry the remains of a large signpost a few feet away.

"So much for 'shoot first and ask questions later,'" muttered Murdox.

The three henchmen watched the signpost glow

with static energy before the largest of the three turned his attention to the little group. He laughed out loud and ripped off his shirt. He craned his neck at an odd angle, and his face began to stretch and twist. His body grew taller, and his muscles bulged outward from his growing skeleton.

The creature's flesh mask fell aside, revealing a nearly seven-foot-tall, savage-looking monster. Its remaining clothes melted away, exposing rusted chain armor that barely concealed its gray skin and coarse body hair. It smiled at the little party with a mouthful of fangs, rotating its jaws from side to side until two prominent lower canine teeth erupted from behind its lower lip.

The remaining two henchmen dropped to their hands and knees and began to shake uncontrollably. They hit the floor, twisting and reeling in long spine-shattering convulsions. They shook and vibrated so fast that their physical forms became almost transparent, and they started to hum like tuning forks.

The beasts within the beasts began to take shape. It started at the head, and then their mouths stretched outward and elongating into muzzles. Then the foreheads began to slope backwards as their ears grew longer and pointed outward at the tips. Their humanoid eyes faded into pools of flowing gold that encompassed the entire eye socket. Their clothing ripped apart and fell away, scattered by the intense vibrations of the violent change.

Their bodies and arms followed, shaking and twisting as they reshaped into new configurations. Finally the spines bent into a curvature, and the beasts' legs drew upward until they took on a distinctly hyena-like appearance. Growing muscles stretched outward over their newly transformed skeletons, and shabby yellow hair grew across their bodies. A moment later they lifted their gruesome heads to the ceiling and cackled wildly at the unseen moon.

"Well, this isn't looking so good for us, is it?" said Murdox.

"I may not be able to see you, but I can still smell you," said the nargoyle as he swung outward with his staff.

The Sentinel easily avoided the blow, side-stepping the attack in order to position himself in the long shadows near one of the walls. The creature sensed his movement and thrust out his staff, jamming it into the wall only inches from Fox's head.

Fox ducked away from the attack, and in a whirling motion the young Sentinel slashed downward with his sword, attempting to break the staff in two. But his strike was stopped dead by the ancient weapon, nearly causing the young elf to loose his grip on his sword from the rebound. Fox shook his hands from the pain.

The nargoyle laughed. "You are a worthy opponent. It has been eons since I've fought such a creditable foe. It will be a pleasure defeating you."

Fox spun on his heels, twirling his weapon around so that it flashed a moment in the dim light before tearing into the soft, leathery skin of the creature's wings. The nargoyle howled in pain and slashed out with its staff in all directions, but Fox was already racing down one of the tunnels that led away from the main concourse.

He had no idea where he should go, only that he had to lead the demon away from the cave. His attack had accomplished two things. The first was to prevent the creature from flying after him, giving him a better chance at a head start. The second was to make the beast angry enough to chase after him. From the sounds of his pursuer's claws tearing into the stone and metal flooring of the ancient train tunnel as it bounded after him, he had succeeded on both fronts.

Before either the goblin or the two hyenas had a chance to regain their composure, Enob grabbed Kase and Murdox and ran with them back in the direction they had just come from. He stopped about halfway down the long tunnel and pulled them up against the wall. "Stay quiet… don't make a sound!" said the wizard. "I'm going to try to get us out of this without getting us all killed."

He whispered into the shadows in an ancient magical language and quietly repeated verses until the darkness around them seemed to deepen. The shadows drew longer and fell all around them like a blanket, hiding them in a pocket of utter darkness.

"This should buy us some time," he said.

Less than a minute later, they heard the thump of the goblin's leather boots on the marble floor as it slowly passed them by. It scanned the shadows with its little red eyes, but Enob's spell seemed to keep them hidden from view. Silently padding behind the goblin were the hyenas. They too scanned the shadows with their glowing golden eyes, gazing right at the trio for a moment but also passing them by without stopping.

The hyenas continued down the tunnel a few steps and then one of them suddenly stopped and turned its head slowly back around in the direction of the little group. The devil-hound began sniffing at the air and cautiously walked back toward them. Then his companion stopped and turned, snuffling at the air and following the lead of the first one.

The goblin also turned on its heels and started poking its mace into the darkness. "Come out, come out, wherever you are…! It seems my pets have picked up your scent."

The hyenas hesitated for a moment in front of the three companions, sniffing at the air and growling into the shadows. Enob grabbed Kase by the shoulder and whispered into his ear. "Let Murdox know that I want the two of you to hold your eyes shut as tightly as you possibly can. No matter what, do not open your eyes."

Kase acknowledged to Enob that he understood and whispered the message into Murdox's ear. A moment later a tiny glow emanated from the palm of Enob's hand, and they all forced their eyes shut as tightly as possible. They ducked their heads toward their chests, shielding their eyes from what was about to come. Then a blast of white light exploded from the wizard's outstretched hand, expanding outward with such force that they could feel the intensity of the blast.

Daylight erupted from the spell, flowing away from Enob and illuminating the darkness as though the sun had risen right overhead. The explosion of light lasted only a few seconds, but that was enough to blind the goblin and the hyenas instantly.

Enob slowly opened his eyes as the light withdrew back into his palm. "You can open your eyes now," said the wizard.

The detectives opened first one eye and then the other, but it was hard to see afterward. Even though their eyes had been shut tightly, the intensity of the blast had been so great that it had still permeated their eyelids.

Kase rubbed his eyes with his fists and squinted in the darkness. "All I can see is stars."

After a few minutes, their eyes returned to normal, and they could see the results of Enob's handiwork. Both the goblin and the hyenas were on their knees, clawing at their eyes and howling in pain. These were creatures of the night, and they probably hadn't seen the light of day in decades, if ever. To be inundated with that much light all at once had nearly killed them.

Enob shook his head. "They'll survive, but they probably won't be bothering us anytime soon."

Fox raced down the abandoned tunnel, jumping from the platform onto the train tracks. He followed the tracks until they led him outside, then quickly tried to gain his bearings. He spotted a hover car parked about a block away, and a plan formed in his mind. The young Sentinel ran to the car and jumped into the driver's seat. He hit the ignition button and somehow managed to fire three of the four ducted fan engines to get the car started.

The craft lifted off the ground listing slightly to

one side, but it seemed to work well enough. He figured that could be sufficient to buy his friends some time.

In a flutter of gray-green wings, the rooftop was swept clean of its aerial inhabitants as the nargoyle stepped from the shadows into a pool of dim moonlight. Its keen, feral eyes peered out into the haze that nearly smothered the abandoned cityscape. Far into the distance it watched, scanning the darkness for the first sign of its quarry.

Within moments it picked up the scent. It howled into the night in defiance, enraged that its wings had been damaged. Nonetheless, the creature leapt off the building, and without fear it fell through the air as the stench of the city rushed passed it.

The nargoyle slammed onto the rooftop of a building nearly fifty feet away, allowing its powerful claws to tear into the concrete and stop its forward momentum. It tested the air once more for the scent of the little elf. Satisfied that it was on the right track, it took off running, leaping from building to building. It was driven by blind fury, and nothing mattered but to find this foe.

A frigid breeze blew across the rooftop of an abandoned building, and the nargoyle stopped in its tracks. It lifted its nose to the sky and breathed in the scents of the city. The prey was close. It snuffled at the air and swished its barbed tail back and forth in anticipation.

The beast leapt off the building and slammed into a parked hover car, crushing in the roof. The windows of the vehicle exploded, spraying glass fragments into the fallen snow. Unfazed by the impact, the demon leapt from the debris and raced off in the direction of its quarry.

The wind was howling, and the snow had started to fall again. It blanketed the front windscreen of the hover car, making it nearly impossible for Fox to see out. He had pointed the craft farther into the city when, *BAM,* his head slammed against the roof. The nargoyle had smashed into the hood of the car, driving it out of control and straight for the ground. Two black voids stared at him from the other side of the windscreen, and the creature grabbed onto the roof of the car as it careened toward the ground.

Fox managed to recover the craft seconds before impact and banked it back up into the sky, forcing the beast off balance. In fury it pounded on the roof of the car and punched in the windshield, spraying glass into the front seat.

It shoved its skeletal head into the cockpit and growled in Fox's face. The young Sentinel slammed on the air brakes, reversing the lift fans and stopping the car in mid flight. The force of the maneuver threw the nargoyle backwards, rolling it off the hood and into the night sky. It fell away from the craft and crashed into the ground in a puff of white snow.

The number three lift fan of Fox's vehicle started to sputter, and he knew he couldn't keep it in the air much longer. He pushed the two remaining engines to their limits, trying in vain to gain as much distance on the creature as possible. That fall might have slowed the nargoyle down, but he doubted it had done any significant damage… probably just upset it more.

The nargoyle leaped to its feet, shaking the snow and glass from its cloak. It howled in defiance at the hover car as it watched the vehicle speed away. In two giant bounds, the creature leapt onto the side of the nearest building and scaled the stone wall.

The number three fan finally gave out, and the remaining two engines didn't have enough power to keep the craft aloft. Fox was forced to bring the hover car down in the middle of a deserted street. The snow was falling steadily again, and the young elf shivered from the cold as snow blew in through the broken windscreen. He tried to fire the number three fan, but it refused to start again.

The Sentinel looked up from the instrument cluster, aware that his keen senses were screaming at him. The creature was close. Fox gazed up into the tall buildings that surrounded him and spotted a dark shape darting from one building to the next, but with the heavy snowfall he lost it from sight.

The nargoyle watched his quarry from his vantage high on the rooftop. He leapt from his perch and dove straight for the wall of a neighboring building. Using his talons to arrest his fall, he dug his claws deep into the concrete structure. Holding onto the wall, he watched the vehicle from above as he clung motionlessly by shear strength alone. Silently he moved closer, creeping along toward his prey like a spider ready to strike from above. He approached to within fifty feet of his target, watching to see what might happen next.

When he saw that his quarry was having trouble with the flying craft, he used this opportune moment to strike. Finally the waiting was over, and he shifted his weight and released his grip from the wall, leaping through the air and landing in a cloud of snow a few feet in front of his victim.

Fox saw the beast hit the ground and didn't hesitate to make a decision. He fired the two remaining lift fans and threw the vehicle forward, straight at it. He crashed into the monster, heaving it up against the broken windshield. The nargoyle's momentum carried it onto the roof, and the creature dug its claws into the thin sheet metal. Four long gashes ripped open over Fox's head, and he pressed the engines forward, but with only two working fans the craft wouldn't climb more than a few feet into the air. It fishtailed back and fourth under the strain as Fox tried his best to bring it back under control.

Left, right, left--the craft skidded and swerved across the road. The vehicle quickly began to overheat and break down. The internal computers tried to compensate for the added demand but couldn't respond in time, and the electrical system fried to the point that the instruments and lighting began flickering on and off. Finally the system gave up and failed altogether.

The vehicle went into a spin and careened across the road and into the side of a building, throwing the nargoyle off the roof and into one of the few unbroken windows that lined the street. Steam and smoke rose from the broken engines, and green fluid leaked into the white snow.

Fox was dazed but unhurt. Quickly he regained his senses and dove out of the car before it exploded. He looked around at the buildings and realized that he had traveled all the way back to the V train station where he and his friends had arrived earlier. A plan formed in his mind, and he checked his watch to estimate whether it could work. After a few quick calculations, he determined that if the train were on schedule he could just make it in time.

The young Sentinel leaped onto the tracks and

raced into the V train tunnel. He arrived at the point where the train accelerated upward into Cloudview, and using the tracks as a ladder he climbed the rungs as fast as he could. He knew the creature wasn't far behind, and from the sound of things it was gaining fast.

As Fox had hoped, the wall directly across from the tracks opened to form a maintenance platform, and he leaped onto the narrow ledge. It wasn't much more than a narrow shelf recessed into the tunnel's wall with a ladder that lead up to the next level of the city, but if his plan worked, it would do nicely.

Fox took a stance at the back of the platform with his back towards the wall. The nargoyle spotted him instantly and leapt to the edge of the platform.

It brandished its weapon and smacked the end of it against the floor. "It ends here, elfling. No more running!"

Fox nodded and looked at his watch… less than a minute to go. The young Sentinel positioned himself in a fighting stance and raised his sword in an offensive posture. The nargoyle didn't waste a moment and lunged forward with his barbed pike. In reaction Fox slid forward and instantly to the right in a fluid, perfectly executed motion. In his passage from one move to the next, he whirled his sword upon a central axis, tracing an invisible sphere in the air. The pike narrowly missed and smashed into the wall where he had been only a moment before.

The nargoyle became furious and yanked the weapon from the wall, swinging it wildly back at the Sentinel; but Fox maintained control over his actions and ducked away from the strike, reversing and retracing his steps and slipping away from every wild attack with relative ease. The nargoyle reacted to every evasion with a new onslaught of aggression, each more deadly than the previous one.

Fox couldn't avoid the pike any longer, and their weapons clashed, echoing loudly through the vertical tunnel. The beast burned with fury and leaped at Fox's throat with its claws. The elf responded by sidestepping the attack and leading the creature's motion into the ground, and once again it missed its mark and slammed into the back wall.

In the distance a whistle blew, and they heard the train approaching from above. The Sentinel stopped in place and waited for the creature to rise. It turned and shrieked at the elf as it lunged forward. It threw all of its might into the attack, as white steam puffed from its nostrils and fire burned in the voids where its eyes should have been. This was no longer a game; the creature had one purpose, and that was to find a way for Fox to die.

An instant before the beast tore into the Sentinel, the elf shifted his body in a spinning motion, whirling to one side and moving slightly ahead of the assault. Inner strength built up in the young Sentinel, and he channeled that energy through his sword and into his attack. The instant the nargoyle slipped by him, Fox slashed downward with his weapon and sliced into the creature's pike. The perfectly crafted elven blade crushed the ancient staff, smashing it into two pieces and throwing a shower of splinters in all directions.

The nargoyle skidded to the edge of the platform and caught itself just before falling backwards into the tunnel. The whistle of the train blew just overhead, only seconds from passing them by. Fox smiled at the creature and spun on his heel, performing a perfectly executed roundhouse kick into the nargoyle's chest. The blow knocked the beast off the platform and into the middle of the tunnel. An instant later the V train whisked by the platform at an incredible rate of speed and slammed into the stony demon.

Car after car whizzed by, and when the train passed, all that remained of the creature was a cloud of dust that floated through the tunnel and made the elf's nose itch.

-Chapter Twenty-

The Wyrd

Drago stood transfixed by the fire pit, watching as the flames danced and swirled just a few feet in front of him. Dragons had a sense about caves, and this one was no different, but he had to admit that this room had been difficult to find, even for him. The room itself was big, roughly rectangular in shape, and very long. The ceiling was vaulted and raised high above the false Sentinel's head, with stalactites crisscrossing the space from end to end.

The most interesting aspect of the cavern was a lake of fire that roiled right in the middle of the huge space. In the midst of that fiery lake was a small island of stone with a pedestal right at its center. The only access to the island was a series of stepping stones that spanned the gap just inches from the flames.

Drago examined the cavern more closely and wandered around the room, ignoring the lake for a moment. The island was surely where he needed to go, and the stones were the obvious choice for reaching it, but he sensed an ancient magic in the room and knew that a trap was about to be sprung.

Kase, Murdox, and Enob descended from the upper levels of the old V Train station and stood at the entrance to the vast cave system beneath. Kase flipped open his backpack and dug out a length of rope, which he tied around one of the many posts that supported the spiraling ramp before lowering it. He shined his flashlight into the dark pit and was relieved to see that the rope made it all the way to the floor below.

After a little complaining on Murdox's part, Kase and Enob managed to convince the wolf-dog that the only way to get him down there was to tie the rope around his belly and lower him down. A few minutes later, Kase and Enob followed, climbing down the rope until they joined him at the bottom.

The pit bottomed out in a circular room, with three tunnels disappearing into the distance. Murdox stuck his head into each of the tunnels, snuffled at the air and scratched at the ground for a few minutes. He finally stopped at the largest of the three tunnels and stood there for a moment. "I'm no bloodhound, but I've got a pretty good nose. I'm sure he went this way."

"I'll mark our way as we go. It'll help us get back out, as well as give Fox a fighting chance at finding us." Kase flipped open his pack once again and pulled out a yellow marker that had ink that glowed in the dark. With it he drew a big arrow that pointed in the direction they were headed. He also dropped an extra flashlight at the edge of the tunnel, just in case Fox had lost his.

All three of them stepped into the tunnel and found that it was large enough for them to stand side by side.

Murdox sniffed at the air. "I'll lead the way. I'm pretty sure I can track him."

For hours they followed the wolf-dog's nose as he led them through a labyrinth of tunnels and vast open caverns. The trail led them across ancient stone bridges that spanned seemingly bottomless pits and through the narrowest of crevasses that would have been impossible to find were it not for Murdox's keen sense of smell. They walked hour upon hour, occasionally having to backtrack up a false trail but never doubting that they were getting ever closer to finding Drago. All along the way, Kase diligently marked little arrows onto the tunnel walls in the hope that Fox would be able to find them.

A few hours into the trip they stopped to take a short break, and Murdox looked up at Kase. "Assuming I can actually find this guy, do we have any sort of idea of how to stop him?"

Kase scratched at the dirt with his foot and twisted his lip at a funny angle. "Well, I haven't actually figured that out...." The young agent looked over at Enob. "Any suggestions?"

Enob shook his head. "Without Fox I'll be forced to fight him with magic alone, and I doubt I'm strong enough to win an outright battle against this foe. If he reads the Wyrd aloud, our only choice will be to use the arrow against him--and we can only hope that my first shot is true."

Murdox growled under his breath and looked back at Kase. "This day just gets better and better. Did you at least remember to bring along the soul-sucker?"

Kase nodded. "Yeah, I brought it with me... but

you know as well as I do that we'd need to get it right up next to him, and I doubt he'll let us do that."

Enob looked very solemn. "For the sake of Eldin's life, and more importantly for the sake of the world, we have to try."

Murdox sat back on his haunches. "You really do like to add a touch of drama to the whole thing, don't you?"

Enob smiled ever so slightly. "I'm a wizard… I wear a robe… its part of the job description."

The little group passed through a magnificent room of pink flowstone that cascaded into a pool of crystal-clear water. Then they entered a vast hall that was too large for their flashlights to find the edges. Massive rock formations formed stalactites and stalagmites that towered from floor to ceiling as far as they could see, and for the first time they all felt a bit insignificant in the world.

Kase looked down at Murdox. "Where now, oh trusty hound?"

Murdox snuffled at the air and paced around in circles for a couple of minutes. "I think we're getting very close."

Murdox wound them between the massive columns on an invisible trail that he alone could follow. It lead them to a deep, dark pit that dropped out under an enormous gap, as far across as they could see. Directly in front of them was a narrow wooden suspension bridge that apparently spanned the gap but ended beyond the range of their lights.

The little party stopped at the edge of the pit. Enob picked up a stone from the ground and tossed it into the darkness below them. More than a minute passed, and even the wolf-dog's keen ears never heard the stone hit bottom.

Enob and Kase looked at Murdox. "So, you're sure he went this way," said Kase.

"Yup, I'm sure," said the wolf-dog.

Enob studied the bridge for a moment. "This is old, but the good news is that it's elven and protected by magic. I'm fairly certain it'll hold our weight."

Murdox snorted slightly. "Oh that just fills me with confidence."

Enob led the way, and they stepped onto the bridge. It jerked up and down and swayed from side to side a little as they walked, but it didn't give way. One by one they crossed over the vast expanse and ended up on a stone ledge carved directly into the sheer rock wall. The only break in the wall was a carved doorway in which hung a large, sturdy, wooden door, with bands of iron crisscrossing the face of it. A charred silver lock, which had at one time latched the door directly to the stone wall, now hung from the door. As their lights shone on the still-smoldering lock, they could see that it had been cracked wide open.

Kase examined the burned lock. "I hope this wasn't the fabled lock you spoke of in your story."

Enob shook his head. "No. This lock has been destroyed with magic."

The wizard pressed against the door, and it swung open on silent hinges. It opened onto a long, perfectly square tunnel that was apparently carved directly through the stone. Light flickered at the end of the tunnel, providing enough illumination to see. They extinguish their flashlights and walked toward the light source.

The false Sentinel watched the flames dance

around the stones just in front of him. As he got closer to them, he could feel the magic welling up in the room and knew without question that something momentous was about to happen. He put his foot on the first stone in the lake of fire, and it began to glow with an intense orange-yellow color as flames climbed higher into the air. With each step he took, the flames became more violent. After the fourth step, he was forced to leap from one stone to the next, because the intensity of the fire became unbearable as it shifted from orange-yellow to an angry red.

Drago leapt across the lake, racing from stone to stone as waves of fire exploded into the air, nearly engulfing him. Somehow he managed to stay one step ahead of the flames. He took one final jump, and as soon as he set foot on the island, the magic in the room solidified into something more tangible. The lake blazed an unearthly color, and its surface exploded in a wave of fire that erupted upward until it reached the ceiling far overhead.

The flames danced across the ceiling, and instead of falling back into the lake, they began to take shape and evolve in front of Drago's eyes. Within seconds the fire swirled high in the air, forming the head of a dragon. The transformation continued in a rippling effect that swelled downward and away from the head. The flames undulated back and fourth along the column of fire as a long, snake-like body formed, extending downward into the lake, where it disappeared far below.

The flame-dragon reared back its head, and two black eyes gleamed into existence. It opened its jaws, and a wave of fire bellowed from its gaping mouth, licking the ceiling far above. Fire danced over the roof of the cavern, charring the rock black with soot, then seemed to dive into the lake below, splashing molten rock in every direction.

The flame-dragon turned its attention to Drago and studied him for a second. "I can see through your camouflage and the false skin you wear… you have the soul of a dragon, little man." It undulated back and fourth in the fire pit and approached to within a few feet of the false Sentinel. "The artifact you seek is for neither man nor beast, but because you are a kindred soul, I will allow you to leave now, relatively unharmed."

Drago laughed at the flame-dragon and withdrew Eldin's sword from its sheath. "I've waited for this moment for eons, and I doubt that an overgrown matchstick can prevent me from accomplishing my goal."

The false Sentinel leapt into the air, swinging his sword in an arc and slicing it across the creature's belly. The weapon tore a long gash into the beast's fiery hide, but an instant later the void filled with fire and the wound disappeared from sight.

"Fool, your weapon cannot harm me!" said the fiery beast. "I am not made of flesh… only flame."

The dragon thrust its head forward and opened its gaping jaws, blowing molten rock and fire from its mouth.

Drago dropped Eldin's sword and dove away from the cone of destruction. He hit the ground tumbling, barely avoiding the wave of fire as it flowed across the island. Tremendous heat radiated from the stone and rocks below his feet, burning his boots and charring his exposed skin.

The fiery dragon turned its head toward the elf and rekindled its attack with another volley of molten rock and flame. The false Sentinel thrust out his hands, and electricity pulsed outward from his palms, enclosing him in a protective force-shield an instant before the wall of fire engulfed him. The force of the blast was enough to lift Drago into the air and fling him across the island where he hit the rocky ground with a bone-shattering thud.

The force of the impact knocked the wind out of the false Sentinel, and his strength was wavering. The impact was enough for him to loose his concentration and control of his magic, collapsing the magical shield. The flame-dragon took advantage of the situation and released another volley of fiery breath.

Eldin's instincts were triggered, and Drago rolled out of the direct path of the blast. The flames spread across the ground like lava, and his elf skin was singed and smoldered from the intense heat. If not for the protection of Eldin's cloak, he would surely have died, but it bought him enough time to cast the magical shield around his body once more, before the flame-dragon could redirect the fiery cone of destruction directly on top of him.

Flames lapped over the protective shield,

heating the sphere of energy until it glowed with an intense orange hue. Drago threw his strength into the magic, and it held against the onslaught of the attack, but his hands began to blister as the intense heat scorched his skin through the magical barrier.

It was a battle of wills, but the flame-dragon gave in first. It circled the pool of flame, snaking its way around the island as it decided what to try next. Drago took advantage of the moment and ducked behind a large boulder to regain some of his strength.

The flame-dragon circled the island like a shark sizing up its prey. Little did it know that this tactic provided Drago the opportunity he needed to take the offensive. The false Sentinel rolled out from behind the boulder and spun around, raising his hands to the flame-dragon. He spread his fingers wide, and black energy rays erupted from his palms.

The dark blasts cascaded around the fiery beast, entangling it in Drago's ancient magic. The creature howled in pain and thrashed violently in the pool of fire. Black smoke rose from the flame-dragon's fiery hide as the magic turned flames into a solid mass. Drago pressed his remaining strength into the magic, increasing the flow of energy in the blasts until he could strain no more. He fell to his knees, his palms burning imprints of his hands into the rocky ground.

The fiery hide of the flame-dragon was burned black, solidified into a mass of rock. Static energy arced over the creature's body, and it reeled in pain, but heedless of its own potential demise, it forced itself to move and once more charged at the false Sentinel.

Drago was on his hands and knees, weak from the battle and the release of so much energy. He looked up just in time to see the creature moving toward him at an alarming rate of speed. He was weak and seriously wounded, but his magic sustained him, and he wasn't willing to give up the fight. He lifted his palms over his head, and magical current radiated outward, enclosing him within an immovable barrier of energy. The flame-dragon collided with the protective shield, and magical power exploded all over the creature in crackling waves of electrical current.

Drago stood firm. The force of the impact was nearly enough to cause him to lose control of the shield, but his magic held, and he managed to maintain it. The flame-dragon pounded into the barrier, striking at the wall of energy and trying desperately to break through its protective fortification.

Drago's arms began to shake under the strain of maintaining the magic, and he felt his strength falter once more. He dug deep into his powers and, by sheer will alone, pressed the magical energy upward, lifting himself from the ground and into a standing position. He threw everything he had left into the enchantment, and his entire body quaked with exhaustion from the strain. The magical barrier grew around him, shifting in color from blue to an intense orange and finally to a fierce red before suddenly exploding.

The wave of pressure blasted outward, cracking the rock floor below him and shaking the walls of the cavern. The flame-dragon was at ground zero of the blast. Energy from the explosion discharged directly into the beast, throwing it upward out of the lake of fire and into the outer wall of the cavern with enough force to knock several massive stalactites from the ceiling. The creature fell to the ground with a sonic bang and burst into a thousand bits of molten rock and stone.

Drago remained at the center of the blast for a moment, allowing some semblance of strength to return to him. His cloak smoldered from the fight, his body was broken, and he was near exhaustion, but he could feel his magic rebuilding, and he knew he could heal this body once more, just as he had done before.

As the companions stepped into the tunnel, they heard a faint whistle from behind them, and they saw Fox racing along the bridge to catch up with them.

The young Sentinel was panting slightly when he joined the group. "Sorry I'm late… that creature chased me halfway across town, but I don't think it will be giving us any more trouble."

Murdox looked up at him. "You've run halfway back across town after defeating a monster that scared the bejeepers out of Kase and me."

"Yes, and I was rather winded. I think I must've gotten a bit out of shape while I was healing," Fox replied.

Murdox shook his head. "You're kidding, right? Well I doubt you could have found a bus coming down here anyway."

Fox smiled. "Well, I did grab a ride on the way in, but it's having some mechanical problems at the moment."

A few moments later they heard a huge explosion, and the walls of the cavern shook. The sound had come from the end of the tunnel, and they followed it cautiously until they emerged inside the flame-dragon's cave.

Drago walked to the stone pedestal and gazed at its smooth surface. In the center of the pedestal was carved a glyph in the shape of the sun, with rays radiating outward from the center. Surrounding the figure was a series of ancient magical signs that glowed a dim green in the cavern light. Drago removed the key from around his neck and placed it into the carved depression of the sun symbol. It matched the carving perfectly and sparkled in the eerie light of the lake of fire.

For a moment nothing happened, but then the key began to glow and turn within the lock until it clicked. The island shook, and the ground began to spiral away into the fire pit of the lake like the shutter of a camera. All that remained of the island was a small circle of concrete that prevented molten rock from flowing into the opening where the island had once been. In the center of the concrete dam was a long spiral staircase, and Drago found himself at the top rung.

The four companions raced to the lake and leapt across the stepping stones until they reached the outer rim of the island. The vault itself was too deep to jump into without breaking their necks, and the interior walls were too smooth to climb down.

Drago was weak, but he managed a vicious smile anyway. "You're just a little too late," said the false Sentinel as he descended the stairs.

Fox was gauging the distance to the staircase and determining if he could make the jump successfully.

"Hold on!" said Kase. If you're going to do what I think you're going to do, you'll need this." The young agent dug into his pack and held up a small black cube that had magical runes carved into each of its six sides. Kase spun it in his hand and pointed to one of the runes. "Trace this character with your finger, and get it as close to Eldin as you can. If it works, the cube will pull Drago's soul out of Eldin's body and trap it inside of itself."

Fox nodded to Kase and took the cube from his hand. He looked over at Enob and said, "If I fail, you know what to do."

Enob nodded to him, then pulled the great ash bow from his shoulder and removed the black arrow from the quiver. The wizard stepped onto the rim of the island and positioned himself as best he could for the greatest vantage.

The young Sentinel took three steps back and turned. He then took a running leap across the stones, hitting the rim of the island with both feet and catapulting himself into the air with all his strength and skill.

Fox soared through the air and dove straight for the staircase. Somehow he managed to grab hold of the metal railing with his hand and swing himself around the structure, leaping onto one of the stairs half the way down.

Drago had already reached the bottom of the stairs and quickly examined the room. He found it to be nearly bare, with no adornments or markings of any kind. The only thing in the room was a small wooden table about fifteen feet from the bottom of the stairs.

Fox hit the bottom of the stairs at a dead run and pulled his sword from its sheath. Drago was just inches from the table, and the apprentice knew he had only one chance to beat the dark force that inhabited his former mentor. He lifted the weapon over his head and flung it as hard as he could at Drago.

The false Sentinel's sixth sense went wild, and he shifted his body away from the projectile an instant before the blade would have hit him. The sword only grazed his shoulder and flew past him, sticking into the wall behind the table and vibrating back and fourth.

Drago smiled and arrived at the table, putting his hand on the sword to steady it. He reached down and picked up the ancient tablet and peered at its surface.

"Noooo...!!"

The false Sentinel slammed the tablet back onto the table.

At the edge of the pit, above the two Sentinels,

Enob held the great ash bow in his hand with the black arrow knocked onto the string. Slowly he pulled the bowstring taut and drew in a deep breath. He focused on his target and concentrated all his attention on Drago. Kase was by that time on his knees, looking down into the pit at the Sentinels, with Murdox by his side.

Kase reach up and touched Enob's side. "Hold on. I think something's happening."

Fox took advantage of Drago's distraction and pulled the black cube from his pocket. He traced with his finger the mark Kase had indicated, and the rune began to glow red. Drago was still preoccupied with the tablet, which gave Fox the opportunity to get closer and to drop the glowing cube at his feet.

Light erupted from the six sides of the device, and Drago turned his attention away from the tablet. The cube glowed an intense red, and all the magical sigils fired at once in a brilliant display of pyrotechnics. A wave of color washed over the false Sentinel, and Drago's dark soul began to be pulled away from Eldin's body.

For a moment the ethereal spirit of the black dragon fought against the energy of the cube, but in the end it was a losing battle. Drago's soul took on the shape of a dragon and tried to escape; but in a tornado of color, the energy of the cube whirled itself around the misty vapor that was Drago and pulled it back down into the magical box.

Eldin slumped to the floor, and Fox rushed to his side and held his mentor's head in his arms. For the first time, he noticed the wounds and burns on his friend's face and hands.

Eldin opened his eyes and looked up at his young apprentice. "Drago... he couldn't read what it said."

Fox nodded to his master. "I have to admit... I never saw that coming."

Murdox glanced at Enob and lightly nuzzled his leg. "Hey, watch that thing!"

The wizard had been so focused on his target that he'd forgotten he still had tension on the bow, and he relaxed his grip on the weapon. Enob looked over at Murdox and started to laugh. He placed the black arrow back in its quiver and slung the great ash bow over his shoulder.

Murdox shook his head for a second and sat back on his hunches and joined in on the laughter. "*Ha, ha, ha*… I guess you would call that poor planning."

"Yes… you would," said the wizard, chuckling uncontrollably with relief.

Kase couldn't figure out what was so amusing. He had heard Drago yell and saw him drop the tablet back on the table, but the next thing he saw was the soul-sucker in action, pulling Drago's spirit from the elf. That had been great, but he wondered what was so funny.

"All right, I give. What are you guys going on about?"

Murdox did his best to quiet down and looked up at the boy. "Don't you see… he couldn't read what was written on the tablet? Drago spent eons of his life searching for knowledge and then for the key and ultimately for the Wyrd. In the end, he did the impossible and found what should not possibly have been found. But everything was in vain. In the end he couldn't read what was in front of him."

The wolf-dog paused for a moment to catch his breath. "Imagine finding a piece of paper with scribbling on it… not letters in any alphabet we know, but rather lines and squiggles, whirls and loops. They wouldn't mean a thing to you without any frame of reference. This was a word written not of this world, in a language that doesn't even exist on this planet in any way, shape, or form. Translation is impossible unless there is some way to decipher what each letter sounds like. In this case, Drago never thought of the translation problem. He might know a hundred or maybe even a thousand different languages, but that did nothing for him. This language and its symbols were completely foreign to him. He sacrificed everything just to discover that it was an utter waste of time."

Kase thought about what Murdox had said. The young agent looked down into the pit and at the tablet that had nearly brought the world to its knees. "Hmmm… I think that's just sad."

"Yes, it is," said Murdox. "Yes, it is indeed."

Below them, Fox helped Eldin to his feet. He was badly hurt, and his body was singed from head to toe, but Drago's magic had already healed him enough that he would survive. Fox stepped to the table and looked at the ancient stone tablet for a second before placing it into his backpack. Then he pulled his own sword from the wall and sheathed it. Eldin limped over to the staircase, and Fox raced to his side to support him. They climbed the stairs together. At Eldin's direction, Fox removed the key from the pedestal, returning the island to the way they had found it.

Enob studied Eldin's eyes for a brief moment. "Glad to see you're back in control of your own body and on our side again," said the wizard.

Eldin nodded and steadied himself against the pedestal. "Glad to be back," he said weakly. The elder Sentinel then looked over the little group. "Thank you for stopping this madness. I tried desperately to break free of Drago's hold, but his will and his powers were just too strong for me. I locked myself away deep in childhood memories and managed to stay hidden. I tried to block him from some information, but his power was so great that he broke down most of the walls I built. In the end I was nothing more than a passenger in my own body, helpless to stop him."

Enob listened to his words, and even without

magic he knew that Eldin spoke the truth. He could see in the elder Sentinel's eyes that this encounter had affected him on a psychological level that would be difficult to overcome. For now the best thing to do was to get him back to Greylok and allow him some time to recover physically, mentally, and spiritually.

The wizard looked over at the younger Sentinel. "So, what do you plan on doing with the Wyrd tablet, now that it's in your charge?"

Fox glanced at Eldin for a brief moment. "I think I can find a safe place for it."

Fox found Eldin's sword at the edge of the island and handed it back to the elder Sentinel. Then they all took a final look at the cave and turned to head for home.

Epilogue

It had been four days since Drago's dark soul had been captured in Kase's magical black cube. Once more Fox found himself on wing flying over the southern ocean through the darkness of the pre-dawn hours. It seemed like an age ago that he and Eldin had crossed this very same expanse in search of an island for the young Sentinel's final test.

He had left Eldin in the capable hands of Greylok's healers allowing his body to recover from his physical injuries. Drago had been the source of the dragon magic that had rejuvenated the elder Sentinel and returned him to his prime. When his dark soul had been vanquished, the magic that kept him young dwindled away and he unwillingly returned to his rightful age.

This, however, was the least of Fox's worries. His friend's body would heal, but it was his mental condition that concerned him. Drago had left him a shell of a man. The beast had violated his mind and body, and he was having a difficult time coming to grips with what happened. He had indefinitely resigned from his senior position as a Sentinel for the kingdom of Greylok, but the King would not accept his resignation easily. Eldin, however, would not relent and he stuck by his decision, forcing the King to give into the man's wishes. This left Fox as the primary Sentinel for the elves, and currently on the most important mission of his short career.

The sun had just broken free from the horizon chasing away the darkness when Fox spotted the small rocky atoll known only as Halfway Island. Stormwise flew over the island in a long lazy circle to determine that all was clear before the great bird tightened her circle and landed on a flat plateau of hard stone.

Fox pulled himself free of his saddle and dismounted from the bird. With a final look around the small island to make sure no unwanted eyes were watching he unfastened the flap on his flight bag. The young Sentinel withdrew a bulky canvas parcel from the pack and pulled away the fabric revealing the stone tablet of the Wyrd. He stared at the alien language inscribed on it, running his finger across the markings. For the briefest of moments he dreamed of the power he held in his hands, but the thought passed from his mind and he pulled the canvas back over the cold stone.

He returned to his flight bag and removed from it a small pouch cinched closed with a leather cord. From it Fox pulled out a small lump of brown clay, which he rolled between his palms until it was round. He placed the clay on the ground in front of him, and with his finger traced a magical sigil into the soft material. Speaking aloud a password that he had created, the Sentinel stood back and allowed the magic to do its work.

The stone under the clay cracked and broke apart disintegrating until a square hole approximately three feet wide by five feet deep had formed. For a moment, Fox examined the hole his magic had created. Satisfied, he picked up the canvas covered tablet and without any hesitation dropped it into the hole with an audible *thud.*

The young Sentinel stepped back from the magical opening and once more spoke his password into the shallow breach. The ground shuddered and the stone knitted itself back together leaving only the lump of clay as proof that anything had ever happened. Fox picked up the clay and crushed it in his fist--completely obliterating the magical ruin. He placed the clay back in its pouch and returned it to his flight bag.

For a final time Fox scanned the island before climbing onto Stormwise's back. He took hold of the flight reins and released their tension while gently prodding the bird in the sides with his heels. The giant bird took off in a run and leapt into the air, quickly leaving the island behind as she climbed out over the ocean.

Fox had successfully completed his first assignment as a Sentinel and he could only imagine what future missions might be in store for him.

Don't miss the next adventure in
the One Wizard Place series:

One, Wizard Place

SIDHE

www.ingramcontent.com/pod-product-compliance
Lightning Source LLC
Chambersburg PA
CBHW051608100726
47898CB00001B/278
* 9 7 8 0 9 8 1 7 4 7 2 0 0 *